The Mum Detective

Gwyneth Rees

MACMILLAN CHILDREN'S BOOKS

First published 2005 by Macmillan Children's Books
a division of Macmillan Publishers Limited
20 New Wharf Road, London N1 9RR
Basingstoke and Oxford
Associated companies throughout the world
www.panmacmillan.com

ISBN 978-0-330-43453-9

9 8

A CIP catalogue record for this book is available from the British Library

Typeset by Intype Libra Ltd
Printed and bound in the UK by CPI Mackays, Chatham ME5 8TD

For Nathan, Zara and Tristan, with lots of love

The morning when it first occurred to me that Lizzie might be going to have a baby, we were all sitting at the kitchen table eating breakfast, except Lizzie, who was standing at the cooker trying to make scrambled eggs. I say *trying* because Lizzie is a rubbish cook and I've had her version of scrambled eggs before, which was why I was sticking to cereal that morning. Lizzie is Dad's girlfriend and she stays the night at our house quite a lot. Right then she was standing side on to me and her dressing gown had come undone. Her nightie had a bump in the tummy area. I stared at it.

'It's a funny time to start work, isn't it?' Dad was saying. It was Saturday, but a few weeks ago Lizzie had started doing an extra Saturday-morning shift at the chemist where she worked. She said that it wouldn't be forever – just for a month or so – and that she didn't have to be there until ten o'clock, which Dad thought was strange since the shop opened at nine.

'Well, they don't get busy until ten,' Lizzie was answering, concentrating on stirring her eggs.

'But you're the pharmacist. What if somebody comes in at nine with a prescription?'

'They have to leave it and come back to collect it later,' Lizzie answered. 'Oh, damn.' She started to prod at the contents of the saucepan.

My brother, Matthew, who was in a bad mood with Dad, reached roughly across him for the butter and nearly knocked over Dad's mug of coffee.

'Careful, Matthew,' Dad said crossly.

Dad and my brother had been snapping at each other since they'd got up. The reason was that Matthew had wanted to go to a party last night with *his* girlfriend – and stay the night there – and Dad had refused to let him do the staying-the-night part. He had driven over to the party himself to collect the two of them – which Matthew reckoned was really uncool – and Matthew had been rude to him in the car, which meant he'd got told off in front of his girlfriend. This was the first time my brother had had a girlfriend and he was keeping pretty quiet about her, despite all my questions. All I knew was that he'd met her in Burger King and her name was Jennifer. He'd been seeing her for three weeks and Dad had met her for the first time last night. I'd asked Dad what she was like, but he isn't very good at giving out detailed descriptions of people, though you'd think he would be since he's a police detective. He told me I would have to wait and make up my own mind when I met her, but Matthew didn't seem in any hurry to bring her back to our house to meet *me*.

Normally Matthew would still be in bed at this time on a Saturday morning but he had promised to do some gardening for one of our neighbours – she was paying him for it – and Dad had insisted on him getting round there on time. 'You know, you'd never have got there at all if you'd stayed the night at that party,' Dad said now. 'And once you make a commitment to somebody, you should keep it. That's what being a grown-up is all about, Matthew.' Matthew is sixteen, four years older than me, so he's not really a grown-up. But he keeps telling Dad that he is and Dad tends to use that against him at times like these.

'You know, you can be really pious sometimes, Dad,' my brother replied.

He can be really rude sometimes, if you ask me. And sometimes, now that he's older, he even gets away with it.

Dad didn't look like he was about to let him get

away with it today though. 'You're heading for a grounding,' he grunted.

'You can't ground me! I'm sixteen! If I lived in Scotland I'd be old enough to get married!'

'That happened in *EastEnders* once – Vicky got grounded by *her* dad,' I informed them. 'And she was *seventeen*.'

Matthew scowled at me. But he soon got his own back because he watches *EastEnders* too. 'That was because her dad thought she was taking drugs, wasn't it? Or was it the time she got pregnant?'

Dad went off on one then. 'I don't know what these TV soap writers think they're doing! They know children watch those shows and what do they fill them with? Drugs and teenage pregnancies! Wonderful! Esmie, from now on, I don't want you watching *EastEnders*.'

'But, Dad, that's not fair! Holly's mum lets *her* watch it.' Holly is my best friend and her mum is really cool – unlike Dad.

'Does she *really*?'

Fortunately, at that moment, Lizzie plonked her plate of toast and scarily rubbery eggs on to the table and said brightly to my dad, 'Maybe this would be a good time to tell them our news. What do you think, John?'

Dad seemed to relax a little bit. He put out his

hand to stop Matthew, who was starting to get up from the table. 'Wait a minute.'

It was plain that Lizzie thought we were going to be ecstatic about their news, whatever it was. I couldn't help glancing down at her tummy and noticing that it was sticking out even more now that she was seated.

Lizzie and Dad had been together for ten months now. Lizzie spent nearly every weekend at our house and two or three evenings during the week as well. I didn't mind because I liked her and she'd been especially nice to me since Juliette, our French au pair, had left two months ago. Juliette had been with us for a year and she was the first person in my life who'd sort of made up a bit for me not having a mum. My real mum died giving birth to me, so I don't remember her.

Lizzie was smiling at Dad. 'Is it OK if I tell them, or do you want to?'

'Go ahead.'

'Well . . .' Lizzie began, and her brown eyes were looking all smiley. 'There's going to be a new addition to the family.'

I gasped. I was right – that was why her tummy was so fat!

Lizzie didn't seem to notice my reaction. 'Wait until you see the photograph.' She grinned at Dad. 'It's upstairs. I'll go and get it.'

She must have had an ultrasound scan. I knew about those because a girl in my class had brought in her mother's scan photo to show us last year, when her mum had been pregnant with her baby brother. I remember looking at it and thinking that the black and white picture looked more like a TV screen that hadn't been tuned in properly than a baby.

I wondered if this meant Dad and Lizzie would get married. I hoped it did. I've always liked Lizzie and I've always been incredibly friendly to her. (Matty says he reckons I'm *so* friendly sometimes that it borders on clingy and that I should give Lizzie more space when she comes round instead of grabbing her the minute she walks in the door and talking to her non-stop. But I don't listen to him since *he* hardly talks to anyone at all when he's in one of his 'needing more space' sort of moods.)

Mind you, I thought now, as we waited for Lizzie to come back, maybe my brother had a point. Holly's aunt had a baby a couple of months ago and Holly says she's never seen anything that takes up as much space as her new baby cousin. It's not the baby itself, she says, it's all its stuff – toys and nappies and feeding equipment and bathing equipment and spare changes of clothes because it's always puking up. Holly said there was something else about the new baby that got on her nerves too – the huge fuss everyone kept making of it. In the end, Holly had told her mum how she felt – Holly's mum encourages her to talk about her feelings no matter how horrible they are – and her mum had made a huge fuss of *her* then, saying that Holly would always be *her* number-one baby, no matter what.

I didn't *reckon* I'd feel jealous if a new baby came along in our family. In fact, I reckoned I'd be pretty excited about it, especially if it was a girl. But if I *did* feel jealous then I guessed I could always talk to Dad – not that Dad likes hearing about my feelings as much as Holly's mum likes hearing about hers.

Lizzie came back into the room and put a photograph on the table. That's when I saw that it wasn't an ultrasound scan at all.

'We know you'd prefer a puppy, but it's not really fair to leave a dog alone in the house all day . . .' She was smiling at me as she showed me a picture of a cute little white kitten.

'A k-kitten?' I stammered. 'But I thought you were talking about . . .' I gulped.

Matthew was grinning. 'I think Esmie thought you were about to tell us you were pregnant, Lizzie.'

'Oh!' Lizzie looked shocked for a moment. Then she laughed.

So did Dad – although his laugh sounded a bit more hollow than hers.

'It's just that your tummy's got really big, Lizzie—' I started to explain hurriedly, but I stopped when I saw the way Dad was looking at me. Lizzie's a bit sensitive about her weight, you see.

'It's all right,' Lizzie said, putting her hand over her tummy, although that certainly didn't hide it. 'I expect it's just this nightdress.'

'Oh no, it's not just that,' I continued. 'It definitely really *has* got bigger because—'

'Esmie!' Dad was glaring at me big-time now.

'You don't have to look at me like that!' I told him huffily. 'Like I'm the Devil's pawn!'

'I think you mean *spawn*,' Matthew said, grinning.

Lizzie let out a little snort and started to laugh and I thought for the millionth time how nice she was. And even though a new baby in our family would have been nice too, at least this way I got to keep Lizzie all to myself.

'So when are you getting this kitten?' Holly asked me as we sat on the bed in her room the following Saturday morning. I had slept over at her house the previous night and Dad was coming to pick me up just before lunch.

'In a few weeks' time, Lizzie says. It's too young to leave its mother at the moment.'

'I thought your dad wouldn't let you have a pet because of him being at work all the time.'

'He says we're only getting it if Matthew and I agree to help look after it, especially me, since I'm the one who wants it the most. He says I've got to understand that a kitten is a big commitment.'

'Lizzie'll help too, though, won't she?'

'Yes, except . . .'

'Except what?'

'Lizzie and Dad haven't been getting on all that well for the last week. I think they must have had a row about something, but I don't know what.'

'How do you mean, not getting on?'

'Well, Lizzie seems to be in a really bad mood with Dad all the time. Like . . . you know how she's a really bad cook? Well, the other night Dad took a lump out of the mashed potatoes she'd made us and left it on the side of his plate – he didn't even complain about it – and she started snapping at him that he could mash his own potatoes in future if he was such an expert. And another time, when he put on a CD, she said she wished he would put on something other than Beethoven for a change. She said she didn't even like Beethoven. She said she preferred The Beatles.'

'I thought she said she *liked* classical music when she answered his advert.' (Dad and Lizzie met through a Lonely Hearts advert – but that's another story.)

'She did!' I answered. 'And she *does* normally. So I don't know why she's getting all grumpy about it now.'

'Hmm . . .' Holly stopped fiddling with her bracelet and sat up straight. She looked like she was thinking hard about something. Holly always seems to find my family life fascinating. She says it's because her own family is more boring in comparison, but that's just not true. OK, so she's an only child, but she's got a great mum who isn't the least bit boring – I've wished millions of times that she was *my* mum – and even though her mum and dad are divorced she still sees her dad lots. (He's a fashion designer, which Dad thinks is a daft job for a man, but then my dad can be pretty sexist about those sorts of things. For instance, he thinks that only girls should wear earrings, which meant it didn't go down very well when my brother got his ear pierced last year. Holly was especially interested when I told her about that, but then she especially loves stories about my family that feature my brother. She's fancied Matthew for ages now – she thinks he's got a bum like Brad Pitt's – and she isn't very pleased about him going out with Jennifer.)

'I wonder if Lizzie wants to marry your dad and he doesn't want to or something,' Holly said matter-of-factly. Holly likes to think that she's a bit of a relationship expert. Her mum is doing a counselling course and Holly is always reading the leaflets and stuff she brings home from that.

'I don't know,' I answered.

'If they're not getting on, they should come and speak to my mum. Part of this course she's doing is about counselling couples who have problems in their relationships. I reckon she'll be really good at it after everything she went through with Dad.'

'Dad says that counsellors and therapists and people like that are only useful if you haven't got any friends to listen to you, and if you're rich enough not to mind throwing all that money away,' I said.

'Well, Mum says having therapy can really help you. *She* says people only make fun of it because they haven't got the guts to do it themselves.'

'Dad's got lots of guts,' I pointed out defensively, 'otherwise he wouldn't be a policeman and go around chasing murderers, would he? Murderers are very dangerous people.'

We were both getting a bit heated about our parents' respective jobs now, and I think we both realized at the same time that we needed to cool it. After all, we were both on the same side, weren't we? I wanted Dad and Lizzie to stay together and so did Holly, because she knows how much I like Lizzie.

'How have *you* and Lizzie been getting on?' Holly asked. 'Do you think she's still upset about you saying she looked fat?'

'She hasn't been acting like she is. I told her I was really sorry and she said it was OK. She even thanked me for making her realize it was time she started a diet.'

Holly looked like a light bulb had suddenly come on in her brain. 'That's it! That's why she's in a bad mood! It's because she's on a diet. My mum always gets really grumpy with everybody when *she's* on a diet.'

'Yes, but Lizzie's not grumpy with everybody – just with Dad.'

'Has he been eating chocolate in front of her or anything like that?'

'No. He's gone on a diet too – to support her. This week he's only been eating *one* doughnut with his morning coffee at work, intead of two, and he's already lost three pounds. Lizzie really glared at him when he told us that yesterday.'

Holly looked like she was continuing to rack her brains for a solution. Then she jumped up. 'Wait here. I've got an idea.'

She came back with two books. One was called *Men Are from Mars, Women Are from Venus*. The other was called *Mars and Venus on a Date*.

'Mum's got loads of books on dating but she says these ones are the best,' Holly said, starting to flick through the second one. 'They tell you all about how men and women are completely different – just as if they were from two different planets. Mum says that's why men and women are always falling out – because they don't understand each other very well so they're always saying the wrong things to each other.' She started to read from a page in the middle of the book. '"If a woman says to a man, *Do you think we are right for each other? Do you still love me . . . ?* what might he say back to her?"'

'How should I know?'

'"He might say –"' she read from the book again – '"*Well, time will tell. That's why we're dating.* Or he might say, *Why else would I be dating you for a year?*"'

I frowned. 'That sounds a bit rude.'

'I know – and this book tells you what he *should* say. "He should say, *Yes, my love for you grows each day I know you better,* or *Yes, I am madly in love with you. You are the most special woman in my life.*"'

I pulled a face. 'Yuck!'

'Well, that's what your dad should be saying to Lizzie and if he's not saying that, then he's getting it wrong!'

'Let me see.' I grabbed the book from her, but it closed in her hand before I could see the page for myself. I opened it again and found myself looking at a whole list of the sort of compliments that a man should give to a woman if he wanted the woman to really like him. They were called *juicy* compliments. Beside it, there was a list of all the sorts of (more boring) things most men say to women, which the book called *plain* compliments. Looking at that, it was easy to see where Dad was going wrong.

I asked Holly if I could borrow a pen and paper so I could write down some of the juicy compliments to show Dad.

At that point, Holly's mum knocked on the door and entered the room. Normally she waits for

Holly to say 'Come in' before she enters, because she's really respectful of Holly's privacy (unlike my dad), but sometimes she forgets. She put down the drinks she had brought us and frowned when she saw the books we were holding. 'What are you doing with those? I've told you before, Holly. The books that I keep in my bedroom are grown-up ones. I don't mind you having a look at them if I'm with you to explain things, but I don't want you just sneaking in there and taking them.'

This is what I mean about Holly having a great mum. I think it's so cool the way she treats Holly – explaining grown-up stuff to her properly so she doesn't get the wrong idea about things. Dad just bans me from reading anything – or watching anything on TV – that he thinks might make me ask awkward questions. But as our au pair, Juliette, pointed out to him when she was here, how am I meant to learn about life if I don't have at least some of my awkward questions answered?

'The books Dad keeps in *his* bedroom are really boring,' I sighed. 'They've got all these boring facts in them about wars and history and stuff.'

Holly's mum laughed. 'Men tend to like facts more than women do, Esmie.'

'Well, I'm glad I'm a girl and not a boy then,' I said, 'because I think make-believe stuff is much better!'

When Holly's mum left the room, Holly and I decided to play a pretend game that didn't involve any facts at all – but because we're too old to be playing pretend games, we called it practising our acting. (We're both in the drama group at school.) I said I would be a woman whose husband was trying to murder her and that Holly should be the detective investigating the case. But Holly wanted to be a relationship counsellor instead and we were arguing about whether relationship counsellors or detectives were better at stopping people from murdering each other, when Holly's mum came into the room again.

'Your dad just phoned, Esmie. Matthew's had a fall climbing up into the loft at Jennifer's house and her father isn't in, so your dad's going round there now. It means you'll have to stay here with us for a while.'

'Is Matty all right?' If Jennifer's dad wasn't in, that meant there wasn't an adult there with them at all. Jennifer doesn't have a mum either, you see, which Holly says is obviously the main reason Matthew is going out with her. Holly once read in one of her mum's self-help books that people get attracted to reflections of themselves. When I'd pointed out that I was pretty certain Jennifer didn't look anything like Matthew, she'd started going on about how the book had been talking about *psychological* reflections – which was where she'd lost me.

'Your dad thinks he might have a broken arm. He's going to take him up to A and E for them to check it out.'

I nodded. The good thing about Dad is that he always knows what to do in a crisis. Accidents and murders especially.

It was several hours later when Dad finally arrived to pick me up on his way back from the hospital with Matthew. Apparently A & E had been really busy and they'd had to wait ages, but eventually Matthew had got X-rayed and it turned out that he'd broken his right arm. The hospital had put it in plaster and given him some painkillers, which must have been really strong because he'd fallen asleep in the car and he didn't even wake up when I got in and slammed my door shut. I'd been hoping Jennifer would be with them so that I could meet her at last, but Dad said they'd already dropped her off at her house.

Lizzie was waiting for us at home and she came rushing out to the car and started fussing over Matthew just like she was our mother. I love it when she acts like that.

Dad got Matthew comfortable in his bed, where he fell straight back to sleep again. I hovered in the doorway for a while afterwards, wondering how mad my brother would get if I drew on his plaster while he was sleeping. I could draw something really uncool like a flower with pink petals. But Dad seemed to guess that I was up to no good because he called to me from downstairs that he had left Matthew's door open so that he could hear him if he needed anything, not so that I could go in there and annoy him.

So I asked Dad if I could go on the Internet to write Juliette an email about what had happened to Matthew and he said that I could, so long as I didn't stay online for long. Dad doesn't really like me using the Internet without a grown-up standing over me – I think he's scared I'm going to meet some weirdo in a chat room or something.

Matty still hadn't woken up when it was time to eat that evening, and Lizzie asked Dad what painkillers the doctor had given him. Being a pharmacist, she knows all about drugs. After she'd looked at the bottle of tablets we'd brought home, she said that he would probably be better off with some painkillers that were less sedating.

'But the doctor at the hospital prescribed *these*,' Dad said.

'I know, but they're pretty strong. I think maybe another type would be better. Why don't you ring his GP in the morning?'

'I think I'd rather follow the A and E doctor's instructions.'

'Fine,' Lizzie said, like in her view it *wasn't* fine. 'So long as you don't expect him to go to school.'

'What do you mean? Of course he's going to school! He's got his exams this year. He can't afford to take time off.' Dad was sounding irritated now, a bit like he used to sound whenever Juliette came up with suggestions to do with us that were different from his. (Juliette and Dad didn't get on very well when she first came to live with us because he reckoned she was interfering too much in the smooth running of our family. The thing is, our family wasn't really running as smoothly as Dad thought – and even he had to admit that Juliette had helped us in the end.) 'Well, he won't be able to stay awake at school if he stays on these,' Lizzie continued. 'And he might still need pain relief, so all I'm saying is . . .'

They went on disagreeing until Lizzie finally snapped, 'Well, he's your son. You do what you want!' Her face was flushed and she said that she thought she'd better go back to her own place tonight because she had a headache.

'Why don't you just go and have a lie-down upstairs for a while?' I suggested, because that's what people always tell me to do whenever I've got a headache.

But Lizzie said it was a really bad headache and that she would have to go.

Shortly after she'd gone, Matthew woke up and said he wanted to come downstairs to watch TV. He's got a portable television in his bedroom, but he wanted to watch *Hollywood's Greatest Action Stunts* on our thirty-two-inch screen. Dad joked that maybe he could pick up some tips on how *not* to break your arm when you were falling out of a loft, but Matthew just pulled a face at him like that wasn't funny.

'Dad?' my brother asked, stifling a yawn when the first advert break came on. 'I've got something to ask you.'

Dad looked across at him.

'It's about Jennifer.' He paused. 'You know how her mum left when she was little? Well, she really wants to trace her. And since you're always tracking down missing people at work, we thought you might be able to help.'

Dad frowned. 'Surely her father's the best person to help her with that.'

'He's already said he doesn't want her looking for her mum. He won't even *talk* to Jennifer about her.'

'Well, this isn't a police matter, it's a family matter. And since it's not our family, I don't think you should be interfering.'

'I'm not interfering. I'm just trying to help.'

'Matthew, what exactly were you looking for this morning in that loft?' Dad asked.

Matthew sighed like he was expecting to have to tell Dad that sooner or later. 'We thought her dad might have put some stuff of her mum's up there. Stuff that might help Jennifer find out more about her.'

'*You* know, Dad!' I burst out, understanding immediately what had given Matthew that idea. 'Stuff like there is in *our* loft!' Dad keeps saying he's going to clear all our mum's stuff out of our loft but, as far as I know, he never has.

Dad was looking serious now. 'I'd be very careful, if I were you, Matthew, before I went behind Jennifer's father's back, digging up the past. Remember, *he's* the one who stayed around all these years and looked after her. He deserves some respect for that, surely. And, anyway, what if Jennifer's mother doesn't want anything to do with her? Have you thought about that?'

'Jennifer thinks she will. She's got this letter from her, see. Jennifer's mum wrote it a few months after she left and her dad gave it to her when she was old enough to read it. She keeps it in this little jewellery box – sort of like treasure or something. Anyway, she showed it to me. It said how much she'll always love Jennifer and how precious Jennifer will always be to her. Stuff like that.' Matthew paused. 'So Jen reckons her mum'll probably be pleased if she gets in touch. She only wants to meet her. She only wants to understand why she left, that's all. She's not expecting to go off and live with her or anything. Come on, Dad! Can't you just help us?'

'By doing what exactly?'

'I don't know. Whatever you normally do to hunt down missing people!'

'Maybe you could put her details into the police computer and see what comes up,' I suggested helpfully.

Dad turned and gave me a look that warned me to keep out of this. But, of course, it was too late for that. I was totally interested now. And there was no way I was going to be able to keep out of it.

When the doorbell rang on Monday afternoon, Matthew and I were having an argument about the television. Holly had come home with me after school and we wanted to watch *Star Trek*, but Matthew had switched over to *Buffy the Vampire Slayer* instead. He really fancies Buffy and he says she looks better on the widescreen than on his portable.

'It's not fair!' I growled at him. 'I've got a friend round and you haven't, so *we* should get to watch what *we* want!' That's always been the rule in our house if one of us has friends in, and Matthew knows it.

Matty started saying that Dad had told him that, because of his broken arm, he could get first choice of what to watch.

'Rubbish!' I snarled. Dad was treating Matthew like he normally did, apart from helping him with stuff that it's difficult to do with one arm in plaster, like washing his hair and tying his school tie. This morning Dad had knotted Matthew's tie for him really neatly, which Matthew had moaned about because normally he only ties it loosely since he reckons it looks cooler that way. One thing Matthew seemed to be managing to do fine on his own, however, was keep hold of the TV remote.

'Aren't you going to answer the door?' Holly asked, when the bell rang a second time.

'Matthew's meant to,' I said. 'With the chain on.' Dad had left strict instructions about how we were to deal with callers in his absence ever since he'd decided that Matthew was old enough to be left in charge of the house and me on school days until he got home from work – unless he was working really late, when he usually arranged for me to go round to Holly's instead.

'I've got a broken arm,' Matthew protested.

'You haven't got a broken *leg*,' I pointed out. 'You can still walk.'

'Maybe it's my mum,' Holly said, jumping up. But Holly's mum wasn't due to pick her up for another hour so I didn't see how it could be her.

We let Holly answer the door and we heard her interrogating whoever it was about who they were, what they wanted and whether they were expected, before she took off the chain. Dad would've been really proud of her.

24

'Who is it?' Matthew and I called out together.

'Jennifer!' Holly shouted back.

I sat up straighter, excited that I was finally going to meet the mysterious Jennifer and slightly miffed that Holly had clapped eyes on her before I had.

Matty immediately sat up straighter too and started using the TV remote to brush biscuit crumbs off his trousers.

'You've got crisps stuck to your jumper as well,' I pointed out to him. And as soon as he put down the remote to pick them off, I grabbed it and switched the TV back to *Star Trek*.

'Come in, Jen!' Matthew called out to her, running his fingers through his hair to make his fringe less flat, because Jennifer had told him it looked trendier when it was sticking up a bit.

Jennifer came into the room, closely followed by a scowling Holly. I quickly saw why Holly was scowling. Jennifer was really pretty. She had a nice face and long blondish hair and she was slim without being skinny. In fact, she reminded me a bit of Rachel, my favourite character in *Friends* – the one who used to be married to Brad Pitt in real life. She was wearing jeans and a cropped blue jumper and dangly earrings in the shape of fish, which Matty had bought for her a couple of weeks ago and that I'd told him she'd never wear because they looked so silly. I saw Holly staring at them as if she thought they were hideous.

'How are you?' Jennifer asked my brother. Jennifer goes to a different school to us so she hadn't seen him since Saturday. She was clutching her mobile and her purse. She looked quite tense. 'I can't stay long. How's your arm?'

'Cool.' Matthew rapped lightly on his plaster, which I still hadn't managed to draw on yet.

'Hi, I'm Esmie.' I introduced myself, since it didn't look like my brother was going to. 'I'm Matthew's sister,' I added, just in case he hadn't bothered to go as far as mentioning my existence to her.

Jennifer gave me a weak smile. 'Hi!' Then she turned back to Matthew. 'Dad's really angry. He says we shouldn't have been up in the loft. He says there isn't any stuff of my mum's up there anyway because she took it all with her when she left. He was really mad at me for going behind his back – and he's mad at you too, Matthew. He says he doesn't think you're a suitable boyfriend for me. I told him I wouldn't stop seeing you and he said I'd have to or else he'd ground me. I've had to sneak over here while he thinks I'm at the shops.'

'Wow!' I gasped. 'This is really romantic! It's just like in *Romeo and Juliet*. They had to meet in secret too, because their families didn't approve. And they ended up getting *married* in secret!'

'Yeah, and then they ended up *killing* themselves in secret,' Holly added.

Matty looked at me impatiently. 'Esmie, can't you and Holly go and do something upstairs?'

I shook my head. 'We want to watch *Star Trek*.'

'Matty wants to watch *Buffy the Vampire Slayer*,' Holly told Jennifer. 'He really fancies Buffy, don't you, Matthew?'

'I just think it's a really cool programme,' Matty replied, blushing.

'Esmie said you nearly bought a poster of Buffy to put up in your bedroom, only you decided to get one of Xena, the Warrior Princess instead,' Holly continued. 'Is that because you fancy *her* even more?'

Fortunately, Jennifer's mobile started ringing at that point and she took the call. 'Hi, Dad . . . yes, I'm at the supermarket . . . No, you don't have to do that . . . Well . . . umm . . . Tesco's, but . . . Dad, wait . . .' She was frowning as she came off the phone. 'Dad's on his way home from work and he thinks I'm at Tesco's, so he's going to come and pick me up from there in twenty minutes. I'd better get down there.' She grabbed her purse. 'Listen, Matthew, from now on we've got to pretend that we've split up, OK? To everyone. Otherwise my dad will find out and he'll kill me.'

Matthew saw her to the front door – his broken arm no longer seemed to be preventing him from walking – and I made Holly sit down with me on the sofa. The sofa is the best seat in our house for watching TV and now that Matthew had vacated it, I reckoned we may as well stake our claim while we had the chance.

I really wanted to watch *Star Trek*, but it was difficult with Holly interrupting all the time to make comments about Jennifer. It was an episode of *Deep Space Nine*, where the teenage son of the captain – whose mother died when he was little – thinks she's come back to life, only it turns out it's not really her but just a clone of her from another space–time dimension. Not for the first time, I let myself imagine what it would be like if *my* mother suddenly turned out to be alive after all. Of course that was impossible, but I found myself thinking about how Jennifer's mother really *could* come back – if only Jennifer could find out where she was.

And that's when I decided that I really wanted to help her look.

By midweek, Juliette still hadn't answered the email I'd sent her on Saturday, so I sent her another one. I was sure that Juliette would have some good ideas about how we could track down Jennifer's mother, if only I could get hold of her to ask her. After all, it had been her idea to put a Lonely Hearts advert in the paper last year to find Dad a girlfriend, and that had worked, hadn't it? I would have phoned her, except that Dad had hit the roof after our latest phone bill arrived. (I'd been phoning Juliette quite a lot since she'd gone back to France – mostly on her mobile.)

As soon as I got home from school on Thursday afternoon, I raced upstairs to the little boxroom Dad calls our study to see if there was an email reply from Juliette waiting for me. Our computer is quite slow compared to the ones at school – Matthew is always moaning about how uncool it is but Dad won't buy another. He says the time it takes our computer to get going is teaching us how to be patient, which is no bad thing, and that the trouble with everybody nowadays is that they expect everything to be done for them instantly.

I was staring at the computer screen, wishing it would hurry up a bit, when Lizzie put her head round the door. She was the only one in the house with me because Dad was still at work, and Matthew was round at his mate Jake's. 'What are you doing, Esmie?'

'Checking our emails.'

'I thought your dad didn't like you going online on your own.'

'Emails are OK.' I looked at her as if I thought she was a bit daft, which is always a good way of knocking her off the scent if she's about to correctly sniff out that I'm doing something Dad wouldn't normally let me do. 'Look. It says we've got six new ones. One of them *must* be from Juliette.' I clicked on the Inbox.

There were five junk ones and one for my brother.

I closed down the mailbox window, feeling cross. It was the first time Juliette had taken this long to answer me. Was she starting to forget about me now? She had said when she left that she'd *never* forget me.

'Esmie, are you OK?' Lizzie asked.

'Yes. It's just that Juliette hasn't bothered answering me yet.'

'When did you write to her?'

'Saturday.'

'Well, that's not very long ago. I'm sure she'll write soon.' She spoke really gently and I thought how Juliette had never spoken gently. She had always spoken quite loudly and bossily. She had said she was only being bossy because she cared about me.

'Lizzie, are you and Dad OK?' I asked. 'You're not going to split up or anything, are you?' It just popped out. One second I was thinking how much I liked Lizzie, and the next I was thinking how much I had liked Juliette and how that hadn't stopped *her* from leaving me.

Lizzie was looking uncomfortable. 'Esmie, I

30

don't think you should be asking me questions like that.'

'Why not?'

'Because that's my business. Mine and your dad's. Listen . . . I came upstairs to ask if you fancied baking some flapjacks with me. I've checked in the cupboard and we've got all the ingredients.'

'*Brilliant!*' I immediately cheered up. (Holly says she thinks it's amazing the way I can cheer up really quickly if I get distracted by something nice, whereas she always feels much more *committed* to *her* bad moods.) 'Holly made some cakes with *her* mum at the weekend,' I added, jumping up. 'But the icing didn't set.'

Lizzie reacted as if I'd said something surprising.

'What is it?' I asked.

'Nothing.' She smiled at me. 'Come on. Let's go and get started.'

We went downstairs and I put on my special apron. A few months ago Lizzie had given me a yellow cotton apron with a red flower embroidered on the pocket, which she'd made at school. She had kept it all these years because she liked it so much and I thought it was really nice of her to give it to me as a present.

'I think we should do more baking together,' I said as I watched her get out a packet of porridge oats and a tin of golden syrup. Nobody ever baked in our house – not even Juliette. She'd always told me that the French didn't rate cakes as highly as the English did because they preferred proper food.

'Well, let's see how these turn out first, shall we?' Lizzie answered.

'Just because you're not a good cook, that doesn't mean you won't be good at baking,' I reassured her. 'So don't worry.'

Lizzie laughed. 'Thanks.'

I got on with measuring out the ingredients. 'Last time I baked fairy cakes at Holly's, Matthew ate nearly all of them when I brought them home,' I said after I'd weighed out all the oats and tipped them into our largest mixing bowl. 'So he's not having *any* of these.' Matthew is a real pig when it comes to eating all the biscuits and cakes and anything nice we have in the house. 'I bet he never stuffs his face in front of Jennifer the way he stuffs it in front of me,' I added bitterly.

Lizzie chuckled and carried on looking in our fridge for the butter. 'Are Matthew and Jennifer still an item then?'

'Oh, well . . . not really, but . . .' Matthew had made me promise not to tell anyone that he was still seeing Jennifer. In fact, Jennifer was coming round to our house this coming Saturday morning when Dad and Lizzie were out at work.

'Does Jennifer still want to find her mum?' I'd

asked my brother when he'd told me that yesterday. 'Because I reckon if she does, she should start by examining that letter her mum sent her as a baby, for clues.'

But instead of taking me seriously, Matthew had asked me mockingly if I fancied myself as Sherlock Holmes, or what? (And that was another reason why I didn't reckon he deserved even *one* of my flapjacks.)

I made sure I was in on Saturday morning when
Jennifer came round. Matthew had tried to get me
out of the house by suggesting I went round to
Holly's, but I'd told him that I'd already invited
Holly round to ours.

'Well, just keep out of our way, OK?' he
instructed me when we were in the kitchen eating
breakfast before either of our guests arrived.

'Don't worry. We're not going to interrupt you
snogging, if that's what you're afraid of.'

'Shut it, Esmie.'

'Shut what?' I asked, opening my mouth and
showing him my tonsils.

'Just shut it,' he grunted again more fiercely.

I gave him a sugary-sweet smile and informed
him that he'd said, *Shut it*, to me eleven times
yesterday. 'Juliette says girls have better language
skills than boys and I reckon she's right.'

He narrowed his eyes. 'Oh yeah? Well, if she's

got such great language skills, it's a shame she can't be bothered to *write* to you any more, isn't it?' He'd heard me moaning to Dad last night that Juliette still hadn't answered my email.

'Shut up, Matthew!' I snarled at him.

'Shut *what* up?' And he opened *his* mouth really wide then, only it was more disgusting to look at than mine because it was stuffed full of soggy toast.

We weren't speaking to each other by the time Jennifer arrived.

'Hi, Esmie, how are you?' she asked, smiling at me as I opened the front door. She was wearing jeans and a short black coat and she was swinging a pink and orange leather bag.

'I'm fine. How are *you*? Is your dad still mad at you?'

'He will be if he finds out I've come here. He's down at his allotment at the moment, so he doesn't know.'

Matthew came thudding noisily down the stairs at that point. I was sure he'd got even louder since he'd got that plaster on his arm. Maybe it made him heavier or something. I knew he would only start yelling at me if I didn't leave them together for a bit, so I went upstairs while they went into the living room. Holly should have been here by now and I wondered if she'd slept in. I was just thinking about phoning her when I heard Matthew and

Jennifer coming upstairs too. At first I thought they had gone into my brother's bedroom, then I heard them talking in the study.

Matthew's bedroom is strictly out of bounds to me – on Dad's orders – but the study isn't, so I went and pushed open the door. 'What are you doing?'

'Trying to find something on the Internet,' Jennifer answered before Matty could tell me to go away.

I squeezed into the space behind Jennifer so I could look across her shoulder at the screen. 'What?'

'The Friends Reunited site,' Jennifer answered.

'Do you think your mum might be on it?'

Jennifer looked a bit surprised.

'Esmie's really nosy. You can't do anything without her finding out about it,' Matthew told her, by way of explanation. 'Esmie, just clear off! There isn't enough space in here for three of us.'

Reluctantly, I left them to it and went to make a start on tidying my bedroom, which Dad had made me promise to do before he got back from work. He had been in a bad mood this morning and whenever Dad's in a bad mood, he always wants Matthew and me to tidy our rooms. I had just started to sort through the stuff on my bedroom floor when the phone rang. I went to answer it in

Dad's bedroom, thinking it would be Holly, but it wasn't. It was Matthew's best friend, Jake. I yelled out for my brother to come to the phone and went back to my own room.

I hadn't been in my room again for more than a couple of minutes when I glanced up to see Jennifer standing in my doorway. 'This is really nice,' she said, looking round. 'I really like your pink wallpaper.'

'So do I, but my friend Holly says it's too little-girly. She says if I had a mum, my room would be more sophisticated because mums have better taste than dads. Apart from *her* dad because he's a fashion designer.'

Jennifer came and sat on my bed. 'Well, I think it's lovely. My room's always been plain cream because Dad doesn't like strong colours. But I think they make the place look a lot cheerier.' I watched her pick up my old Barbie doll from the window ledge. (I never play with her any more, but I'll never get rid of her because she once belonged to my mother.) Jennifer started to try and untangle Barbie's hair, which is a bit frizzy because she's so old. I told her about my gran giving me my mum's Barbie, and Jennifer said that the only thing she still had of *her* mum's was a half-knitted baby cardigan with the knitting needles still attached.

'How come?'

'Dad says she was knitting this cardigan for me but she never finished it because she tripped down our front steps and broke her arm when she was pregnant.'

'Oh, that's a . . . a shame . . .' I mumbled, suddenly feeling awkward because we were talking about Jennifer's mother who had abandoned her.

'You wouldn't say that if you saw the cardigan,' Jennifer joked. 'It's lime green.' She pulled a face.

I smiled. 'I guess it must be difficult to knit when you've got your arm in plaster.'

'Yup! In fact, Matthew was complaining about that only the other day!'

I giggled and the conversation got easier after that. Jennifer said that she had some photographs of her mum, but that she wasn't allowed to put them up in the house. She also said how much she liked the photograph on our mantlepiece of my mother (when she was eight months pregnant with me) and Matthew.

'Your mum looks really huge in that picture!' she said, smiling.

I nodded. 'Dad says I was quite a big baby. That's not why she died though,' I added quickly. 'I came out fine. It was afterwards that things went wrong. They couldn't stop her bleeding or some-thing.' I don't normally talk to people I don't know very well about how my mother died, but I guess I felt like I could trust Jennifer because she had confided in me about *her* mother.

'I'm sorry,' Jennifer said.

'It's OK.' I never know what to say when people say they're sorry about my mum. I mean, of course it's not OK that she's dead, but then it's not *their* fault, is it? 'So did you find your mum on the Internet?' I asked her quickly.

She shook her head. 'She hasn't registered on the Friends Reunited site. I checked her maiden name as well as her married name.'

'Doesn't she have any relatives who might know where she is?'

'She had a sister called Helen, but Dad says they'd lost touch by the time he and my mum got married.'

'How come?' I found the idea of sisters losing touch with each other very strange indeed. I mean, I can't ever imagine losing touch with Matthew, no matter how much of a pain he continues to be when we're both grown up.

'I only know what I managed to get Dad to tell me when I asked him ages ago. He said my mum and her younger sister were brought up by their grandmother because their mother left when they were little and their dad couldn't cope with looking after them on his own so he left them too. When they grew up, Mum's sister went to university to study to be a doctor and their grandmother was really proud of her, but my mum dropped out of college and their gran didn't approve of that at all and there was a big argument. Soon after, their grandmother died and my mum refused to go to her funeral and my mum and Helen didn't speak after that.'

'That's terrible!' I gasped.

Jennifer just nodded as if she didn't feel anything much about it at all. I thought it was really odd the way she had told the story – as if she was telling me about some people who had nothing to do with her. But then I suppose she hadn't actually known any of them, had she? Not even her own mother.

I thought about how I'd never known *my* mother either. But the difference was that I've always thought of *my* mum as still being with me, sort of looking down on me. Sometimes I even talk to her when I'm in bed at night. So you see, she's always been a part of my life even though she's dead. And I've always known exactly where she is.

'Do you think it's true that your dad really doesn't have any contact details for your mum's sister?' I asked Jennifer now. The first step in being a good detective, I reckon, is never to assume that people are telling you the truth. They hardly ever are in any of those detective programmes you see on TV, and Dad says they often aren't in real life either, although it might not be because they've murdered anybody.

'That's what he said.'

'Maybe he only said that because he doesn't want you to find her. I think you should check to see if there are any old address books in your house. There might be an address for your aunt in one of them.'

'Dad's only got one address book and I've already looked through that,' Jennifer said. 'Thanks for trying to help though, Esmie.'

'Thanks for being nosy, you mean,' my brother said, coming to join us.

I turned on him angrily. 'At least I've *got* some ideas about how to find Jennifer's mum!' I snapped. 'Unlike *you*!'

'Actually, Matthew had an idea too,' Jennifer put in quickly. 'My mother wrote me a letter when I was a baby, see, and Matthew reckoned we should look at that more closely for clues!'

'Oh, *did* he?' I glared at my brother.

'Yes,' Jennifer continued. 'So I brought it with me to show him, and we had a look at it just now. There's no address on it, of course. I'd have checked that out long ago if there was. So—'

'Maybe there's a postmark on the envelope,' I interrupted excitedly. 'Then at least you'd know where she posted it.'

'There isn't an envelope. Dad only kept the letter.'

'Oh . . . well . . . can *I* see it?' I asked.

'Hark at Miss Marple,' Matty said drily. 'One look at that letter and she'll crack the case straight away!'

'Maybe I will—' I began, but Jennifer interrupted *me* then.

'This isn't a joke, Matthew,' she said sharply, getting up abruptly and walking out of my room.

Matthew rushed after her. I know I should have let them have their privacy and all that, but I couldn't stop myself following them. Jennifer had gone back into the study. Matthew went in too and put his arm round her shoulders, saying that he knew it wasn't a joke.

'All we want to do is help you, Jennifer,' I called out from the landing, 'because we know what it's like not to have a mum!'

Matthew started to yell at me to go away, but Jennifer stopped him.

'It's OK,' she sniffed. 'I'm sorry. Esmie's right. You *are* helping. Here . . .' She picked up her pink and orange bag, unzipped it, and pulled out a folded piece of cream writing paper, which she handed to me. It looked like it was quite old. 'You can see her letter if you want, Esmie.'

I opened it up carefully. It was written in printed

capital letters, the way my grandmother in Bournemouth used to write to me when I was little so that I didn't have to decipher her funny joined-up handwriting.

DEAR JENNIFER, it said, I AM WRITING THIS LETTER FOR YOU TO READ WHEN YOU ARE OLDER SO THAT YOU KNOW HOW MUCH I LOVED YOU AND HOW PRESCIOUS YOU WILL ALWAYS BE TO ME. She had spelled the word 'precious' wrong – with an extra 's' in front of the 'c'. I noticed because I always used to do that too and my English teacher was always crossing it out with her red pen. I used to have trouble with 'vicious' and 'gracious' as well.

I didn't point out the spelling mistake to Jennifer. I just carried on reading. PLEASE REMEMBER I WILL ALWAYS LOVE YOU, it ended.

The doorbell rang then and my brother hissed, '*Don't* go blabbing all this to Holly!'

'Of course not!' I snapped, feeling annoyed at having to leave them – and the letter – before I'd completed my assessment.

I had only just opened the front door when the phone started ringing, so I dashed into the living room to pick it up while Holly took off her coat.

It was Dad, wanting me to look up the number of the chemist shop where Lizzie worked. He said she wasn't answering her mobile and he needed to know if she wanted to go with him to a fortieth birthday party that he'd just remembered he'd been invited to tonight.

'OK, Dad. I'll go and look for the number and ring you back,' I said. I came off the phone and raised my eyebrows at Holly, who had already sat down on our sofa. 'I don't know why Lizzie bothers having a mobile. She always has it switched off.' I couldn't think where the phone number for Lizzie's shop was at first, then I remembered that she'd written it on a piece of paper and stuck it on the fridge door. I went and got it and phoned Dad back straight away, but his phone went straight to voicemail.

'Why didn't you just leave him a message?' Holly asked when I put down the phone without leaving one.

'If it's something important Dad likes me to make sure I speak to him in person. He's always forgetting to pick up his messages.' I tried his number again but it was still going through to voicemail.

'Try him again later,' Holly said.

'I'll forget if I leave it,' I said. 'I know, I'll phone Lizzie at the shop and then *she* can phone him back.'

Holly went off to make herself a drink in the kitchen.

'That's weird,' I told her when she came back.

'What is?'

'I just phoned the shop and Lizzie's not there. The woman who answered says she never works there on Saturdays.'

'I thought you said she worked there every Saturday morning now.'

'She does, but the person I just spoke to said Lizzie hasn't *ever* worked there on a Saturday. But I don't understand because she *goes* there every Saturday!'

Holly and I stared at each other. If Lizzie wasn't going to work, then where *was* she going? And where was she now?

'Let's try her mobile,' Holly suggested. 'She might have it switched on by now.'

I picked up the phone again and dialled Lizzie's mobile number, and we immediately heard a muffled ringing tone.

'She's left it *here*!' Holly started to lift cushions off the sofa until she found Lizzie's phone under one of them.

I hung up and the mobile stopped ringing. I went over and took it from Holly. I could see there was at least one message on it as well as the missed call from us. I stared at Lizzie's phone. You must never

ever listen to someone else's private voice messages. I know that. It was just that now Lizzie wasn't where she was supposed to be, I felt like I absolutely *had* to find out where she really was. Even if that meant doing something I knew was wrong. Before I could change my mind, I pressed the button that lets you hear the messages. It asked me to key in a pin number before it would let me listen to them, but that wasn't a problem since Lizzie uses the same four-digit pin number for everything and I know what it is. I listened to the message at the other end, expecting it to be from Dad. It wasn't. It was from a man whose voice I'd never heard before. The message had been left this morning at just before ten o'clock, which was the time Lizzie had told us she had to be at work today.

'Hello, Lizzie,' the voice said. 'This is Andrew. I'm afraid I've had to take my dog to the vet as a bit of an emergency. I'm on my way back to the house now and I should get there in about ten minutes. See you then!' He had a very smooth, quite posh-sounding, English accent.

I handed the phone to Holly, who listened to the message too. 'He sounds a bit like Hugh Grant,' she said. (Hugh Grant is Holly's second favourite actor after Brad Pitt. Holly likes older men, in case you hadn't noticed.)

I was frowning. 'I've never heard her talk about anyone called Andrew. I wonder who he is.'

Holly gave me a knowing look, and I instantly knew who *she* thought he was.

'Don't be daft!' I exclaimed indignantly. 'Lizzie can't be . . . *you know* . . .'

'My dad was,' Holly said. 'He was seeing that stupid Tara for six months before Mum found out.'

'But Lizzie wouldn't do that!'

'You did say that your dad and Lizzie haven't been getting on that well lately,' Holly continued. 'All I'm thinking is—'

'Well, don't think it!' I snapped angrily. And I stomped out of the room.

I knew there had to be a simple explanation. I couldn't believe Lizzie was having an affair like Holly had suggested. Holly's dad had two affairs at different times while he was married to her mum so I could understand that being the first explanation she would think of. But Lizzie wasn't like Holly's dad. Lizzie was . . . well . . . *Lizzie*.

I couldn't think why she would need to keep her meeting with this Andrew person a secret, and I couldn't think why she'd told us she was going to work at the chemist on Saturdays if she wasn't. But I trusted Lizzie enough to believe there was a perfectly innocent explanation for both of those things.

That is, I trusted her until the telephone conversation I had with Juliette a couple of hours later. Holly had had to go home for lunch by that time and Jennifer had gone too because she wanted to get home before her dad got back from his allotment. I was just thinking about sending Juliette another email, even though she *still* hadn't replied to mine, when this horrible thought popped into my head. What if Juliette had had an accident and that was the reason she hadn't replied? The more I thought about it, the more I reckoned that Juliette could quite easily have had a car accident. Just before she'd gone home to France she'd said she was going to have to keep reminding herself to drive on the *right* side of the road again because she'd got so accustomed to driving on the *wrong* side in England.

'You mean the *left* side, Juliette,' I had said, but Juliette had informed me that the left side *was* the wrong side as far as she was concerned. She'd added that she was looking forward to driving on the correct side again in France, but that she was going to have to be careful not to have an accident while she was getting used to it.

Now that I was imagining Juliette driving the wrong way round a French roundabout and crashing, I knew I had to speak to her immediately, no matter what Dad said about the phone bill.

I rang her number and her mother answered. '*Âllo?*'

'*Bonjour. C'est Esmie,*' I said in my best French. '*Je désire parler avec Juliette, s'il vous plaît.*'

Juliette's mother, who speaks very good English

but still always likes it when I talk to her in French, asked me how I was. Then she went to fetch Juliette.

'Juliette!' I was so excited to hear her voice again that I immediately forgot that I'd been imagining her lying in a hospital bed a few minutes earlier. She told me she'd just got back after being away for a week with some friends. We chatted for a bit and she asked after Matthew and Dad and Lizzie, then I told her what had happened today. When Juliette lived with us, I told her everything and it was hard to get out of the habit.

Juliette sounded cross. 'Really, this is too much, you listening to this message on Lizzie's phone. You should not be doing this! This sort of behaviour can only lead to trouble.'

'Sorry,' I mumbled sheepishly. 'But Juliette, listen . . . Holly says Lizzie's probably having an affair. But she can't be, can she? I'm just going to ask Lizzie who Andrew is as soon as she gets in.'

'Be careful, Esmie.' Juliette sounded worried.

'Why?' I asked. I had expected her to agree with me that Holly was just being silly.

Juliette was silent on the other end of the line but I knew she was still there.

'*You* don't think she's having an affair, do you?' I asked sharply.

'I did not say that.'

'Well, if she's *not*, then it doesn't matter if I ask her who Andrew is, does it?'

'That depends. It may be that she has been keeping him secret for some other reason.'

'Like what?'

'I don't know. Like perhaps . . . perhaps . . .' It sounded to me like she was struggling to come up with any alternative explanation.

Before Juliette had time to say anything else, the front door slammed and I heard Lizzie in the hallway. 'HELLO-O! Is anybody in?'

'It's Lizzie,' I said. 'I'm going to go and ask her right now if she's having an affair!'

'Esmie—'

'I'll speak to you soon, Juliette. Check your emails cos I've sent you two.' And I put down the phone.

Matthew had already made his own lunch and taken it up to his bedroom, where he was listening to music, so I had Lizzie all to myself as we made sandwiches together in the kitchen. She asked me what I'd been doing this morning and I know I should have asked her then what *she* had been doing – and checked out whether she was going to lie to me – but, when it came to it, I couldn't bring myself to trick her like that. So instead I blurted out straight away, 'We rang you at the shop this morning and you weren't there.'

'What do you mean?' Lizzie had her face turned away from me because she was filling up the kettle. That was poor detecting tactics on my part. You should always ask your suspects questions when they're looking at you. That way you can tell from their faces whether they're lying or not, unless they're really good liars, in which case you might need to use a lie detector to help you – except that Dad says they don't have any of those in British police stations.

'We had to ring you because Dad wanted to ask you something and you weren't answering your mobile.' Now that I was telling her this, I remembered that I hadn't phoned Dad back yet and that he hadn't phoned me back either. 'So I phoned the shop and a lady answered and said you weren't there.' I decided not to say the bit about Andrew yet. I reckoned it would be better if *she* told me about him first.

'Who answered?'

'Someone called Mary.'

'And what did she say to you?' Lizzie still wasn't looking at me.

'That you didn't work there on a Saturday. But I don't understand because you've been going there every Saturday for the past month.'

'Mary must have made a mistake,' Lizzie said, turning to face me now.

'But why would she do that?'

'I don't know. Maybe she got me muddled up with someone else.'

'So you were there all the time then?'

She nodded. 'That's right.'

'But what about Andrew?' I blurted it out before I could stop myself. 'You left your mobile here and I . . . I . . .' I flushed, but there was no going back now. 'I listened to his message.'

Lizzie looked flustered. 'I knew I'd left my phone here but . . . What did he say?'

'He said he was going to be late home because he'd had to take his dog to the vet but that he'd meet you there in ten minutes.'

'Let me hear it.'

I went and got her phone and watched her face very carefully as she listened. All sorts of scary thoughts were starting to whizz round my head, like what if Holly was right after all? What if Lizzie *was* having an affair?

'Andrew must have made a mistake,' Lizzie said after she had finished listening. 'I'd better ring him.' I thought her voice sounded a bit shaky, but I might have been imagining it. Dad says that feeling suspicious can make you imagine things about people sometimes, which is why it's very important for a detective to always keep an open mind.

'But who *is* Andrew?'

'Oh, he's . . . he's just an old friend I've arranged to meet *next* Saturday morning. He must have got the dates muddled up and thought I was going to see him today. I'd better ring him straight away.' She started to walk out of the kitchen with her phone and I followed her.

'But you work on Saturday mornings,' I pointed out.

'Well, next Saturday I've . . . I've got the morning off.' She turned round and spoke to me quite sharply then. 'Esmie, stay here and finish your lunch!' She carried on upstairs and I heard her go into Dad's bedroom and shut the door.

I guessed she was annoyed with me for listening to her private phone messages. But at least her explanation for everything *had* been reasonable. Sort of. She had a *friend* called Andrew. Well, that was fair enough, wasn't it?

Lizzie stayed upstairs for ages. I got bored waiting for her in the kitchen and went through to the living room to watch TV. The phone started ringing soon after that and I waited for someone else in the house to pick it up but nobody did.

'Hello?' I answered. (I used to say our telephone number when I answered the phone, but I don't ever since Holly pointed out that it might be some weirdo on the other end who's only phoning to say rude words or do heavy breathing. She read somewhere that people like that just punch in telephone numbers randomly until they get one that works, which means they don't actually know what number they've called, which means it's really stupid to reel it off to them because then they can make a note of it and call again.)

'Esmie? Is Lizzie there?' It wasn't a weirdo. It was Dad.

'She just got back. Dad, I tried to phone you but I got your voicemail, and then I tried to phone Lizzie at the shop but—'

'I know. I've been on the phone all morning. Something's come up at work and I'm going to be caught up for the rest of the day. I've decided to give this party a miss. I should be home later this evening but there isn't much food in the house. I wanted to ask Lizzie if she could pop out and get something.'

'I'll go and get her,' I said. I went upstairs and realized why Lizzie hadn't answered the phone herself. The bathroom door was shut and when I called out to her, she called back that she was washing her hair. 'Dad's on the phone,' I shouted through the door. 'He says he's not going to be home until late and he wants you to get some shopping.'

'OK,' she called back. 'I've got my mobile in

here with me. Tell him to hang up and I'll ring him back.'

I went downstairs again and told Dad what Lizzie had said. 'What is it that's come up at work, Dad?' I asked. 'Has there been a murder or something?' I've become a lot more interested in Dad's work since I've started thinking that I might like to be a detective too when I grow up, but Dad still won't tell me much about it. Instead of answering me he asked if I'd tidied my room yet, and when I said that I was still working on it, he told me I'd better get back to it. Then he said, 'See you tonight, sweetheart,' and hung up.

When I went upstairs, I could hear Lizzie talking to him on her mobile in the bathroom, but I couldn't hear what she was saying. I wondered if she was telling Dad about her friend Andrew leaving a message on her phone and me listening to it. I hoped she wasn't, because if Dad found out I'd done that, I was going to be in trouble. Dad is always saying I've got to learn that I can't just go around invading other people's privacy whenever I feel like it. (When I recently pointed out that detectives do that all the time, he said, 'Not without a search warrant, they don't,' and carried on giving me a huge row because he'd just caught me nosing around looking for love letters in Matthew's bedroom.)

Still, at least if Lizzie was telling Dad about Andrew, it proved that he definitely couldn't be her secret boyfriend. I thought about how – unlike Holly and Juliette, who had let their imaginations run away with them – I had kept an open mind and looked for a sensible solution to the mystery. And I thought how *that* proved I would make a totally brilliant detective!

On Monday, Matthew was meant to be looking after me until Dad got home, but at five o'clock Jennifer rang him and asked him to go round there. Her dad had phoned her to say that he was going straight to his allotment after work to do some weeding, which meant they'd have her place to themselves.

'I'm not supposed to leave Esmie,' I heard my brother say. 'Can't you come here instead?'

She said something and he said, 'Right, well OK, but I won't be able to stay that long.' As he put down the phone, he picked up a pencil that was lying by the messages pad and poked it down his plaster to scratch at the skin.

'Dad said it would just get even more itchy if you kept doing that,' I warned him.

'Yeah, well it's not Dad's arm, is it?' Matthew grunted. 'Listen, Ez, you don't mind staying here on your own for an hour while I go round to

Jennifer's, do you? She can't come here because she's got to make dinner for when her dad gets back.'

'You're not allowed to leave me in the house on my own,' I reminded him.

'Yeah, but that's just Dad being overprotective. We don't have to tell him.'

'I want to come with you.'

'But, Esmie—'

'If you go without me, I'm telling Dad,' I said, which I knew would end the argument. I didn't really have any objections to being left in the house on my own but I was keen to see Jennifer too, and I was especially keen to find out how her search for her mother was progressing.

Matthew knew he had no option but to take me with him, though he hardly spoke to me for the whole walk round to Jennifer's house. I guess he thought it was really uncool, having his little sister tagging along with him.

Jennifer looked surprised to see me when she opened her front door – though not horrified, which I guess Matthew would have looked if the situation had been reversed.

'I had to bring her,' Matty said quickly. 'She wouldn't stay—'

'That's OK,' Jennifer interrupted him, smiling. 'I think it's really sweet the way you look after Esmie.'

'*Sweet?*' My brother looked perplexed. That's because he hasn't got a clue how the female mind works, which he would have if he read one of Holly's mum's magazines. A few weeks ago in *Cosmopolitan* there was a survey where they showed lots of women all these pictures of different men, and some of the men were holding babies and some weren't. Eight out of ten women found the men with the babies more attractive. *Cosmo* said it was because women like it when men show their caring sides. I guess that probably extends to big brothers showing their caring sides too.

I could tell Matthew was going to ruin everything by saying something horrible to me any second, so I quickly intervened. 'Matty never leaves me in the house on my own, do you, Matty?' Don't ask me why I was helping him. Maybe it was because I had taken a liking to Jennifer and I wanted her to keep on being his girlfriend. Or maybe reading that *Men Are from Mars* book at Holly's had kick-started me into automatically trying to save *everyone's* relationships.

Fortunately, Matthew seemed to realize at that point that he was on to a good thing and, instead of answering me back, he just smiled nonchalantly as if it took him no effort at all to be the most caring big brother in the whole world.

Jennifer led us upstairs to the spare bedroom,

where they kept their computer. It was already switched on. 'I've been checking out some more Internet sites. I wanted to show you one of them. Look.' She typed 'missing persons' into the Google search and came up with several agencies that claimed they could locate missing people for you for a fee.

'Isn't it really expensive?' I asked, thinking that these people must be private detectives, and the only private detectives I had ever seen were ones on TV programmes who always charged their clients loads of money per day – plus expenses.

'It depends how easy the person is to trace, but they do it through database information and stuff. Anyway, I've got some money in a savings account and I can use that. Look. This is the one I think looks the best. It says they trace missing relatives as well as bad debtors.'

'Bad debtors?'

'People who owe you money and don't want to be found.'

Matthew and I read the site's home page. It sounded straightforward enough. You just had to give them all the names the missing person might be using, their last known address, their approximate age and anything else you knew that might be helpful in locating them, like what they might be doing as a job.

'My mother's name is Catherine Joanne Mitchell, or Catherine Joanne Forbes if she's using her maiden name,' Jennifer said. 'This house is her last known address – 2 Acacia Avenue – and she'd be forty-one by now.' She paused. 'But I have to give them my contact details and email address and I think I might have to pretend that I'm over eighteen. I was wondering if you could do that from your computer, Matthew. That way they won't be sending me back any messages that Dad might see.'

'Sure.' Matthew picked out a pen from the pot on the desk, scribbled on his plastercast to check it worked, then asked for a piece of paper so that he could write down the website address. 'Do you know what she might be working as or anything like that?' he asked.

Jennifer shook her head. 'She was studying English at college before she dropped out – that's all I know.'

'Maybe she went back to college—' I started to say, but just then we heard the front door open.

Jennifer gasped. 'Dad's not meant to be back yet.'

She went out on to the landing while Matthew and I stayed in the spare room, holding our breath. 'I thought you were going to your allotment after work, Dad,' Jennifer called down the stairs to him.

'The police have cordoned it off. Probably kids down there taking drugs or something.' He sounded annoyed. 'Whose coat is this in the hall?'

I gulped. I had left my jacket over the end of the banister. Matthew had dumped his on the sofa in the living room.

'Have you got a visitor?' We could hear Mr Mitchell's footsteps coming up the stairs now.

I suddenly realized the computer screen was still showing the missing-persons site. 'Quick,' I hissed, pointing at it. 'We've got to switch it off.'

While Matthew struggled to close down the computer in time, Jennifer was trying to stall her father. 'It's Esmie's coat,' I heard her say.

'Esmie?'

'Matthew's little sister.'

Mr Mitchell was outside on the landing now and, before he could come into the room, I rushed out to join Jennifer. My heart was beating really fast, but her dad hadn't said anything about her not being allowed to see *me* again, had he? Mr Mitchell stared at me. He was a big man – taller and broader even than *my* dad – and he had thick dark-grey eyebrows and grey hair. He didn't look very friendly.

I quickly shut the spare-room door behind me and that was a mistake. If I'd had a bit more experience as a detective I would have known that when you don't want to draw attention to something, the best thing to do is to act like you don't have anything to hide. But I shut the door like I *did* have something to hide and Mr Mitchell cottoned on immediately and pushed past me to open it. He caught Matthew just as he was trying to fit himself inside the wardrobe. My brother had knocked one of Mr Mitchell's suits off its hanger in the process and was trampling it underfoot as he attempted to close the wardrobe door with his good hand.

'WHAT THE HELL DO YOU THINK YOU'RE DOING?' Mr Mitchell roared at him.

I don't know how Matthew felt but I nearly wet myself.

Matthew scrambled out of the wardrobe, nearly tripping as his feet got tangled up in Jennifer's dad's trousers. His face had turned the same colour as a very ripe tomato. I hadn't seen him look so embarrassed since the time he forgot to lock the bathroom door and Holly walked in on him just after he'd got out of the shower. (He was standing stark naked with his back to her, looking in the bathroom mirror and trying to squeeze a spot on his chin. It was soon after that that Holly started going on about him having a bum like Brad Pitt's.)

Mr Mitchell was turning to face Jennifer now. 'I thought I told you I didn't want you seeing this boy again!'

'I know, but *I* wanted to see him, Dad. I asked him to come round. I—'

He didn't wait for her to finish. He whirled back to face my brother again. '*YOU!* OUT! OR I'LL GIVE YOU MORE THAN A BROKEN ARM TO WORRY ABOUT!'

That really scared me. I ran down the stairs, grabbed my own coat and fetched Matty's from the living room. Matty came thudding down the stairs after me with Jennifer's father close behind. Matty and I both dived out the front door and didn't stop running until we were out of Acacia Avenue and back on the main road.

'Not even Dad shouts as loudly as that, does he?' I said, panting to get my breath back.

'Not at you, maybe,' Matthew replied. 'He can turn up the volume pretty high when he's laying into *me*.'

I frowned. I still didn't reckon our dad was anywhere near as scary as Jennifer's. I mean, Matthew and I both knew that Dad would only ever go so far when he was angry with us. But we didn't know that about Jennifer's father, did we?

We got home to find a long, angry message on our answerphone from Mr Mitchell, telling Dad that he didn't want Matthew going anywhere near

Jennifer from now on. Matthew instantly wiped it off the machine.

'Dad'll be cross if he finds out you've done that,' I told him.

'Yeah, well, I'll take the risk. This way he might not find out anything. Oh, damn.' Matthew was looking at his watch.

'What's wrong?'

'Lizzie said she'd drop in a chemistry book she reckons is really cool. She was going to bring it round today on her way back from work. I hope we haven't missed her.'

'Does Lizzie know about chemistry then?' I asked. This was news to me. It hadn't occurred to me that our potential stepmother might come with additional bonus features.

'Of course! She's a pharmacist, isn't she? She *works* in a chemist's.'

Matthew needn't have worried because it was half an hour later when Lizzie arrived with the chemistry book under her arm. I invited her into the kitchen and told her I was going to put the kettle on because I'd made some more flapjacks and I wanted her to taste one. Before she could protest that she hadn't been meaning to stay, I was laying out two teaplates and two teacups on the kitchen table and getting out the teapot.

'Are you having tea too, Esmie?' she asked. 'I thought you didn't like it.'

'I don't, but I'm trying to acquire the taste. Holly says it's easy to acquire the taste for things if you persevere long enough. She's done it with coffee, black-cherry yogurt, olives – but only the green ones – and vegetable pakora.'

Lizzie laughed. 'Well, this is very nice. Thank you.'

I put the flapjacks out on a plate in the middle of the table and folded two pieces of kitchen roll in half to make napkins. Then I made the tea and offered her a flapjack, which she bit into straight away and pronounced delicious.

'So is your friend Andrew an old friend from college or university or something?' I asked, picking up a flapjack myself.

She looked surprised. 'No, not from university. I met him . . . later than that.'

'How long is it since you last saw him?' I continued. (After further discussion with Holly at school, I had decided to carry out some further interrogation – or *supplementary* interrogation I reckon you might call it if you were a detective.)

'I don't know, Esmie. A while.'

I decided I'd better come straight out with my main question before she lost patience with me. 'Is he an old *boyfriend*?'

'No!'

And just then I thought of another really important question – one that hadn't been suggested by Holly. 'Did *he* locate *you*?'

'How do you mean?'

'Well, if you'd lost touch, how did he find you again? Was it through the Internet or something? Like on Friends Reunited for instance?'

She frowned. She had stopped eating her flapjack. 'Esmie, why all the questions?'

I had suddenly switched to thinking about Jennifer's mum and how, even though we didn't have any clues to help us find her, we did have a clue that might help us find her *sister*. Her sister was a doctor – and Lizzie was a pharmacist, which meant she knew more about doctors than I did, because they were always writing out prescriptions and sending them to her. 'Lizzie, if there was a person you wanted to find who was a doctor, how would you do it?'

She looked at me sharply. 'What makes you think Andrew is a doctor?'

'Huh?' I was confused for a moment. Then I remembered that she hadn't realized I'd switched subjects. 'Oh – I'm not talking about *him*. I'm talking about—' I broke off abruptly. I couldn't tell her about Jennifer's mum without breaking confidentiality, which is something a good detective should never do. 'How would you do it, that's all?'

Lizzie was looking at me warily. 'If you want to locate a medical doctor, you can look up their name in the medical register.'

'What's that?'

'It's a list of all doctors in the UK, with contact addresses for them.'

'Where would you find the medical register?' I was starting to feel excited.

'It's on the Internet now, I think, and they have it in book form in the reference section of the library. But, Esmie—'

'I've got to go now,' I interrupted, deciding I'd better get out of the kitchen before *she* started firing awkward questions at *me*. 'I've just remembered I've got homework to do.' And I grabbed another flapjack and rushed out of the room.

At school the next day, there was a rumour going about that a dead body had been found on the local allotments, and everyone who knew that my dad was a detective was asking me about it. When I confessed to Holly that this was the first I'd heard of it because Dad hadn't mentioned it to me yet, she was very unimpressed.

'What's the point in having a dad who's a detective if you can't get any inside information on murders?' she asked.

'Dad never tells us about his work,' I told her. 'You know what he's like.'

'Yeah, but I reckon you could do more snooping around than you do. I mean, he must bring paperwork and stuff home with him sometimes, doesn't he? Can't you sneak a look at that?'

'I've never seen him with any paperwork. I think he keeps everything in his office.'

'Well, can't you find out *something* about this?

Can't you at least find out if the body's a man or a woman?'

'I don't see how.'

Holly sighed, like she reckoned I was a lost cause. 'Well, don't tell this lot you don't know anything. Just pretend you know all about it but you're not allowed to say anything because of confidentiality reasons.'

After that, when people started asking me stuff, Holly nearly always gave them an answer before I could. Before the day was over there was one rumour going about the school that *three* bodies had been found, and another that the murder weapon was a spade that belonged to somebody on the allotments. And both rumours had been started by Holly.

After school I asked Holly to come to the library with me (I didn't want Dad to know that I was looking in the medical register and I was afraid he would find out if I used the Internet at home). I had already told Holly that Jennifer was trying to locate her mum without her dad knowing, and sworn her to secrecy about it. On the way to the library, I told her about Jennifer's aunt being a doctor and what Lizzie had told me about finding doctors.

'I think it's really interesting that you're so keen on finding Jennifer's mother,' Holly said. 'I reckon it's because *you* haven't got a mother that you're doing it.'

'Huh?'

'Mum told me about this lecture she went to the other day about how some people are sort of *psychologically programmed* to seek out the missing relationships in their lives. And with you, that's a mum, isn't it?'

'I'm not searching for *my* mum! I'm searching for Jennifer's!' I protested.

'Yeah, but I bet you wouldn't be so excited about finding Jennifer's mum if you weren't sort of *programmed* to search for mothers in general.'

'Shut up, Holly! You don't know what you're talking about!' Holly's psychobabble – as Dad calls it – really winds me up sometimes. Dad says it's not Holly's fault and that she gets it from her mum, but then he would say that, since Holly's mum has always – especially since she started doing her counselling course – been able to wind *him* up.

'I do know what I'm talking about,' Holly replied firmly. 'And listen . . . you know how you want to be a detective when you grow up? Well, I reckon, because of the way you're *psychologically programmed*, you'd make a really good *mum* detective – one who specializes in finding missing mothers. What do you think?'

'I think you're crazy.'

Holly shook her head. 'I'm just unusually perceptive for a twelve-year-old. That's what Mum says.'

I nearly answered that my dad thought she was unusually *precocious* for a twelve-year-old, but I decided to keep quiet because we had just arrived at the library and I wanted Holly to help me look for the book. I felt a lot more confident doing this with her than I would have doing it on my own.

'Lizzie said it would be in the reference section,' I told her. Inside the library I started to look up and down the shelves, not really knowing what I was looking for. It was Holly who marched straight up to the desk and asked a librarian. (Holly and her mum always go straight up to assistants in shops and places and ask to be directed to the thing they want. When Juliette was here, she used to do that too, but only because she said English shops were too disorganized for her to be able to find anything by herself.)

'What did you say that book was called again, Esmie?' Holly shouted to me, which was embarrassing because you're meant to keep quiet in libraries and that made everyone look at us.

'The medical register,' I said, keeping my voice to a whisper as I came over to join her. 'It's a book that lists all the doctors in the UK.'

The librarian pointed to a section headed Y for

Yearbooks. I'd never have thought of looking there. I'm like Dad in that I always like to find things by myself and I always spend ages looking for stuff before I'll give in and ask anybody. I dreaded to think how long it would have taken me to find this book under Y for Yearbooks, rather than M for Medical.

Holly and I pulled out the four volumes of the medical register that were there. They looked like big dictionaries. We started to flick through them and found that, inside, the doctors were all listed in alphabetical order. There were quite a few doctors who had Forbes as a surname. I skimmed through them until I came to those whose first names began with H. There were three Helens. One was a Helen Anne who had qualified in 1988. I did a quick calculation in my head. Jennifer had told me her mother would be forty-one years old now, which meant that Helen – if she was, say, two or three years younger – had to be in her late thirties. In 1988 she would therefore have been in her early twenties, which sounded about right for graduating from university. Helen Anne Forbes had an address in London, which I quickly copied out.

The next Helen Forbes had no middle name and had qualified in 1991. I supposed that could be her as well. Her contact address was a surgery in Birmingham, so I wrote that down too.

The last Helen Forbes had qualified in 1955,

which meant she was far too old to be the one we were looking for.

'What are you going to do now?' Holly asked as we left the building together.

'I'm going to write to both of them, giving *my* address, and explaining that Jennifer is trying to get in touch with her mum.'

'Why don't you get Jennifer to write the letters? She can still use your address if she doesn't want any replies to get sent to her house.'

'I'm not going to tell Jennifer yet,' I answered firmly. 'That way, if I don't get any replies, she won't have her hopes raised for nothing, will she?' There was also another reason why I didn't want to tell Jennifer. I was afraid that, if I told her, she would tell my brother and then they would want to do everything else by themselves. And the thing was, this had been my idea – my lead – and I wanted to see it through to the end.

Holly and I walked back slowly towards the part of town where we lived, not talking much. I was thinking about what I should write in the letters. When we were almost at the place where we had to go our separate ways, Holly suddenly asked, 'Has Lizzie told your dad about Andrew yet?'

I looked at her in surprise. I thought she'd forgotten about that. 'Yes, I told you. He's just a friend. Women can *have* male friends, you know.'

'That's what my dad said to my mum at first, when one of Mum's friends first saw him in a restaurant with Tara.' Holly's voice cracked as she said Tara's name and I thought – not for the first time – that underneath all the flippant comments, Holly was a lot less cool about her parents' break-up than she was always making out.

But I knew from experience that Holly would snap my head off if I suggested that, so I just said, 'Yeah . . . well . . . this is different.'

'Why?'

'It just *is*.'

There was an awkward silence between us for a few minutes. I was afraid Holly wasn't going to let the subject drop, but when she spoke again it was about something different. 'When are you getting your kitten? You haven't talked about it in ages.'

I felt my stomach knot up, because the reason I hadn't talked about it – and had been trying not to think about it – was that Lizzie had told us during the week that her friend had decided to keep all the kittens because her kids had got really attached to them. Apparently, there were only three in the litter and she had three children who had each chosen one as their special pet. So we were going to have to look elsewhere if we wanted a kitten our-selves. But when I'd asked Lizzie *when* we were going to start looking elsewhere, she'd said it was up to Dad because it was his house and it would be his kitten.

'I'm sure when Dad and Lizzie first said about getting a kitten they meant one that would be Lizzie's as well as ours,' I told Holly now. 'That was definitely how it sounded.'

Holly frowned. 'Are you sure they're not thinking about splitting up?'

'I don't know.' My stomach felt even more knotted up.

'Did you try telling your dad about that *Men Are from Mars* book?'

'It's not that easy. He hasn't exactly been *asking* for my advice, you know.'

Holly looked thoughtful. 'Are you still coming round to mine next weekend?'

I nodded. Holly's aunt and her aunt's new baby were staying with her next weekend and Holly wanted me to come and see her new cousin. 'I've got to ask Dad, but I'm sure it'll be OK.'

'Maybe we could smuggle the book out of Mum's room again and you could take it home with you. Then you can just leave it somewhere where your dad'll see it. He might start reading it by himself then.'

'I suppose,' I said, not thinking it was very likely that he would. Self-help books aren't exactly Dad's thing. Like I said before, he prefers to read books about battle strategies or how engines get put together.

'Though of course that won't help much if Lizzie's already having an affair.'

'I told you! She's not!' I growled. 'So stop saying that!'

I carried on walking to my house after we'd parted, and when I got there I was surprised to see Dad's car already in the driveway. He was never usually home this early. I rang the bell because I can never be bothered to get out my door key if somebody's in, and Matthew came to the door. It turned out that Dad's car was only there because he hadn't been able to get it started this morning, so he'd had to go to work in a taxi.

'That case he's working on has been on the news. Someone found human remains in the allotments,' Matthew told me, grinning. 'Isn't that cool? Oh – and it gets better! Jennifer just phoned and she says her dad's hopping mad because the police have sealed off the whole area and he won't be able to get to his vegetables until they've finished with it!'

'Wow! Did they show any pictures on television?'

'The reporter guy was standing in front of the allotments while he was speaking. There were some police in the background, but not Dad. I suppose he might get on the telly later if he has to make a statement.'

'Did they say anything about the body? Everyone at school was asking me about it.'

'Only that some poor guy who'd just taken on an overgrown patch of ground was doing some digging and he dug up a bit of old clothing. Then he dug a bit deeper and found it!'

I went upstairs to get changed out of my school uniform, wishing that I could go down to the allotments and see all this for myself. But I knew I wouldn't be allowed to.

I sat down at the desk in my bedroom and pulled out a blank sheet of notepaper from the box of flowery stationery I'd been given last Christmas. I was keen to write letters straight away to those two doctors, one of whom I hoped was going to turn out to be Jennifer's aunt. But what should I write? I started by printing my address and phone number very clearly in the top right-hand corner. Then I wrote the following letter:

Dear Dr Forbes,
You don't know me but I got your address from the medical register in the library. I am trying to find my friend's aunt who is called Helen Forbes and is a doctor. She might have got married and changed her name. My friend (who's called Jennifer) is trying to find her mother and she thinks her aunt might know where she is. Her mother's name is Catherine. Jennifer hasn't

seen her mum since she was a baby and she would like to contact her. If you can help, please write back to me or phone.

I thought for a minute or two about how I should sign it. Then I wrote:

Yours sincerely,
Esmerelda Harvey

I thought putting my full name made the letter look more official.

I read the whole thing through, then copied it out a second time for the second Helen Forbes. Then I wrote the addresses on the envelopes and put a first-class stamp on each one before going down to the postbox on the corner of our street to post them.

While I was doing my homework, Lizzie arrived. She had brought the ingredients to make chilli con carne, which is one of the few things she can actually cook quite well. Dad apparently knew she was coming and had promised her that he'd be home in time to eat it.

Dad *was* home in time – just – and it was lovely to have all of us sitting round the table like a proper family with a mum as well as a dad. After Dad had taken his first forkful of chilli, he told Lizzie it was nice – which I noted was only a *plain* compliment, not a *juicy* one. So I said it was *really delicious* and that Lizzie was *really talented at making chilli con carne* to demonstrate the sort of compliments he ought to be making. Dad grinned at Lizzie and nodded as if he agreed with me, so I reckoned that at least counted as him sort of *upgrading* his compliment to a juicy one.

As we ate, Matthew started asking Dad questions about the body on the allotments. 'Can you tell how long it's been there?'

'We're still working on that. It's not as easy to age skeletal remains as they make out on those TV detective programmes, you know.'

'So, it's just a skeleton then? Like . . . there's no . . . *flesh* and stuff?'

Dad pointed to his dinner and frowned at my brother. 'Do you mind?'

'Do you know how it was murdered?' I asked, as Dad shovelled in a big mouthful of chilli.

Dad carried on chewing for a bit, then he grunted, 'Like I said, Esmie – it's difficult to tell at this stage.'

'But is there a bullet hole in the skull or anything like that?' I persisted. As Matthew sniggered, I turned on him crossly. 'If you knew anything about being a detective, you'd know that you should always look for the obvious first when you come across a body. Isn't that right, Dad?'

'Esmie, do you mind if we move on to a more cheerful subject?' Dad said, pointing to my heaped plate of food. 'A bit less talking and a bit more eating would be good.' He turned to my brother, who had nearly finished his dinner, and asked, 'So how's the studying going, Matty?'

I concentrated on eating my dinner, and listened while Matthew moaned to Dad about school and all the homework he'd been given.

Then, when I reckoned I'd been quiet for long enough, I said, 'Dad, can I go round to Holly's at the weekend? Her baby cousin's going to be there and Holly says she's really cute.'

'I don't see why not, sweetheart. I don't think we've got anything planned for Saturday or Sunday yet, have we, Lizzie?'

'I'm meeting my friend in the morning on Saturday. That's all.'

'That's right,' Dad said. 'Why have you got the morning off again?'

'They want to use the shop for some training.'

'Oh, that's right, you told me. So what time are you meeting her?'

'Ten o'clock.'

'Lizzie's friend isn't a *she*, it's a *he*,' I put in, when it didn't look like Lizzie was going to correct him. 'He's called Andrew. But don't worry, Dad. He's not an old boyfriend because I already checked.'

Matthew let out a muffled snort.

'*What?*' I demanded, glaring at him.

Lizzie had a half-amused expression on her face as she looked at Dad. 'I won't be gone long.' She turned back to look at me. 'Maybe I'll come and visit Holly's cousin with you afterwards, Esmie. I like babies too. We ought to buy it a little outfit or something.'

'Cool!' I said, grinning at her.

I really liked Lizzie a *lot*, I decided. And if Dad didn't end up marrying her, I was going to be very upset about it indeed.

Two days later Lizzie met me from school on her half day so that we could go shopping for baby clothes together.

When I was younger I used to imagine what my mother would look like standing at the school gates and it had always involved her having just been to the hairdresser's and looking much prettier than all the other mums. For a couple of seconds I let myself imagine that Lizzie was my mother. Her hair was looking a bit messy, but it didn't matter since she was sitting inside her car and, anyhow, now I'm older I know that looking pretty isn't the most important quality in a mum. (And I know that being a good cook isn't the most important thing either – even though it would be nice if Lizzie learned to cook *something* other than lasagne and chilli con carne.)

'People probably think you're my mother,' I said when I climbed into her car.

'Surely they won't think I'm old enough,' Lizzie teased me as she started up the ignition. 'I expect they think I'm your sister.'

'You reckon?' I said, pulling a disbelieving face. Lizzie laughed.

'Where are we going to look for a baby outfit then?' I asked. 'There's this really trendy shop in town that does great clothes. I think they do baby clothes too. Juliette took me there to get a dress for Holly's birthday party last year. Remember I put it on to show you the first day you came round to our house?'

'I remember. It was a lovely green colour, wasn't it? You looked beautiful in it. But I think that shop is a bit expensive.'

'OK.' I reckoned Juliette would have gone back to that shop no matter how expensive it was because she always says that the English don't spend enough money on clothes and that's why they're not nearly as well dressed as the French. But, come to think of it, that time she'd taken me there, she *had* been spending Dad's money rather than her own.

We ended up going to our local department store and choosing two really cute little Babygros and a set of bibs with teddy bears on them. Afterwards, I asked if we could stop and have tea in the cafe on the top floor, because Holly's mum always takes her there (unlike Dad who will *never* stop for tea in town, because he says it just prolongs the agony of shopping). Lizzie had started to say that we could buy some nice cakes to have with Dad and Matthew when we got home instead when she saw my face and seemed to change her mind. 'Come to think of it, it would be nice to have a sit down. And they do very good coffee here.'

I beamed at her and we took the escalator up to the cafe and stood in the queue, where I spent ages looking at all the different cakes before deciding on a chocolate eclair. I had an orange juice to drink with it and Lizzie got a coffee. While she was waiting with the tray to pay at the till, I went and got us a table.

We chatted about all sorts of stuff as we sat there. I ended up telling her that I wanted to be a detective like Dad when I grew up and she told me that when she was my age she wanted to be an astronaut. I said, 'Yes, but I really *am* going to be a detective.' And she laughed and said, 'Good for you!'

After we'd finished our drinks, we went to the greetings-cards department to buy some wrapping paper and, while I was choosing some, Lizzie went to have a look in the bookshop section next to it. She found something there that she brought across to show me. It was a box and book set that had a picture of a detective holding a magnifying glass and the words CRIME-BUSTER KIT on the front. The little pocket-sized book gave you tips about how to solve crimes and the box contained bits of detectives' equipment. There was a very cool detective's ID card, a little magnifying glass, a pair of plastic gloves, some sealable plastic bags with EVIDENCE printed on them, a little plastic pot with a scew-on lid, which I guessed you were meant to use to collect samples of *liquid* evidence (like spilt blood), a tiny square ink-pad for taking people's fingerprints, and a stick of chalk to use for drawing round dead bodies.

'It's not expensive,' Lizzie said. 'Shall I get it for you?'

'Oh, yes please!'

I started to read the book on the way home, which wasn't a great idea because I always feel sick if I read in the car, but fortunately we got home without me having to use one of my evidence bags to puke up in.

By the time Dad got back from work, I was just finishing taking Lizzie's fingerprints like it showed you how to do in the book. I'd tried to take Matty's as well, because the book said you should try and build up as big a database of fingerprints as possible, but he'd told me to get lost when I'd asked him.

'What's all this then?' Dad asked, watching as I rolled Lizzie's last finger from left to right on my little ink-pad, then repeated the action on the sheet of paper I was turning into a fingerprint record sheet.

'Lizzie bought me this great book that shows you how to be a detective,' I told him. 'It's really cool. It tells you how to take fingerprints and how to check if something's forged – like a letter for instance.' I released Lizzie's hand and pointed to the unopened letter Dad had picked up from the hall.

As Dad opened it I immediately seized the envelope to examine it under my magnifying glass. The first thing I looked at was the postmark. 'This was posted locally,' I announced, moving the glass down over the name and address, which were both written by hand in block-capital letters. MR J. HARVEY, I read, peering closely at the writing. The letter 'A' wasn't written like an ordinary capital 'A', I noticed. It was written like this:

MR J. HaRVEY.

All the capital 'A's in our address were written like extra-large little 'a's. I was just about to start deducing whether the handwriting looked more like a man's or a woman's, when Dad grunted, 'Go and tell your brother I want to see him, please, Esmie.'

'Why?' I asked. 'Who's the letter from?'

'Just do it.'

'What is it, John?' Lizzie asked as I left the room.

Out of the corner of my eye, I could see him showing the letter to her. 'It's from Jennifer's father.'

I raced upstairs and knocked on Matthew's door, yelling excitedly, 'Dad wants to see you in the kitchen. He's just had a letter from Jennifer's dad! I think you're in trouble!'

'*What?*' Matthew came and flung open his door. 'What does it say?' He was looking worried.

'I don't know, but Dad doesn't look too pleased.'

As he followed me downstairs, Matthew started muttering the sort of stuff he always mutters when he thinks he's about to get into trouble with Dad – that he was sixteen, for God's sake, that Dad could just butt out of his life for once, and that he was damned well going to tell Dad that. I just went, 'Yeah . . . sure . . .' because I knew that once he got face to face with Dad, there was no way he was going to dare mouth off at him.

Dad was speaking on his mobile in the kitchen and it sounded like he was going to have to go back in to work straight away. (For once, Matthew looked relieved instead of irritated at that.) Lizzie wasn't in the kitchen, so I guess she'd decided to opt out of this particular family battle.

Dad ended the call, slipped his phone into his pocket and picked up the letter from the table. 'Perhaps you could enlighten me about this,' he said crisply, looking at Matthew like he was a prime suspect in a major crime. (I reckon it must be really scary having Dad interrogate you if you're a murderer.) Dad slowly read out Jennifer's father's letter. '*Dear Mr Harvey, I am writing to ask that your son, Matthew, does not come to my house or see my daughter again. In my opinion, he has shown himself to be an unsuitable companion for her. Firstly, he tried to enter my loft without my permission – this was his idea and my daughter unfortunately went along with it. A few days ago I caught him sneaking about behind my back in my house, causing damage to items of my clothing. I am also afraid that he is causing emotional distress to my daughter by deliberately stirring up upsetting feelings about her mother. My daughter is very precious to me and I will not stand by and allow this to happen. I therefore hope that you can ensure that he stays away in future. Yours sincerely, Alan Mitchell.*' Dad looked up at my brother. He was frowning. 'Well?' he demanded.

'I don't know what he's talking about,' Matthew said defensively. 'I haven't damaged anything of his.'

'So what are you saying? That he's making this up?' Dad sounded impatient.

'Maybe he means when Matthew trampled all over his suit,' I pointed out helpfully.

'You *trampled* on his suit?'

'Not on *purpose!*' Matthew said, giving me a sideways glare.

'Matty was hiding in the wardrobe and he knocked it off its hanger,' I added, to make things clearer. 'And then he sort of trod all over it, but he didn't mean to. It was an accident.'

'You were hiding in a *wardrobe?*'

Matthew flushed. 'I knew Jennifer would get into trouble if her dad found me in the bedroom with her so—'

'You were in the *bedroom?*'

'Esmie was there too! We were on the computer. But I knew he'd freak out if he found me because he'd already said I wasn't to go round there again.' He swallowed. 'But I had to Dad! I had to see her!'

'You see, it's just like in *Romeo and Juliet*—' I started to explain, but Dad gave me a look that made me think it was wiser not to make that comparison right now.

'Why does he want you to stop seeing Jennifer?' Dad demanded.

'Because he's a—' Matthew broke off from saying whatever rude word he'd been going to say as

Dad frowned at him. 'Well, it's not fair, Dad! I haven't been stirring up any feelings about Jennifer's mum! She talks to me about her because she can't talk to *him*. She *asked* me to help find her!'

Dad looked stern. 'But it's *his* house, Matthew, and if he doesn't want you in it, you should respect that!' He glanced at the kitchen clock. 'I think I'd better phone him before I go into work and try and straighten this out.'

'NO!' Matthew burst out.

Dad ignored him and went through to the living room, where Lizzie was watching TV. 'Is everything all right?' she asked.

'It will be,' Dad said, making for the phone.

'Dad, you don't know what he's like! You'll just make it worse if you phone him!' Matthew protested.

'We can't leave things like this,' Dad said firmly. 'Now, what's Jennifer's number?'

Matthew shook his head. 'I don't want you to phone him, Dad.'

'What's the number?' Dad repeated, in the special voice he uses when he's not going to ask nicely again.

Matthew knew he had no choice but to give in.

I held my breath as Dad phoned. Matty had gone pale. Lizzie pretended to be still watching TV with the sound turned down, but I could tell she wasn't really.

'Jennifer, is that you?' Dad said into the phone. 'This is Mr Harvey – Matthew's dad. Can I speak to your father, please?' There was a pause, then he asked, 'Well, when are you expecting him back? . . . OK . . . Well, will you tell him I rang and that I'll call him tomorrow?' He came off the phone and looked at Matthew. 'He's out for the evening. But I *will* be phoning him back.'

Dad looked at his watch, turned to Lizzie and pulled an apologetic face. 'I'm afraid I've got to go back into work, but I shouldn't be more than an hour or so.'

'You've got to work *again*?' Lizzie sounded irritated and I hoped they weren't going to have an argument about it. I reckoned Lizzie ought to understand about Dad's work better than most people, because her father had been a policeman too.

The two of them went out to the hall together and Matthew darted out of the room as well, which left me alone. Dad had left the letter from Mr Mitchell on the coffee table, so I took my magnifying glass out of my pocket and picked it up to examine it more closely. I decided that, if Jennifer's father was a crime suspect, I wouldn't need a handwriting expert to identify his writing because of the way he used those funny capital 'a's. He had printed his address in the top right-hand corner of the page and the 2 ACACIA AVENUE bit had four weird-looking 'a's in it. As I was scanning the rest of the letter, I noticed something else too. The word *precious* was spelled wrong. It was spelled *prescious* – with an extra 's'. Just like in the letter Jennifer had got from her mum.

I had got out my detective book and was reading the section on examining written evidence when Lizzie came back into the room, looking harassed. She said Dad's car wouldn't start again so he had taken hers and she was going to phone Dad's breakdown service to get them to come and have a look at his. She'd intended to go home since Dad was going to be working this evening, but now she couldn't because she'd had to lend him her car. She looked down at the magnifying glass and the letter I was still holding and asked me what I was doing.

'Nothing,' I said, quickly leaving the room and taking them with me. I headed upstairs, where I met Matthew on the landing. He was wearing his outdoor jacket.

'Has Dad gone?' he asked me.

I nodded. 'His car wouldn't start again so he had to take Lizzie's. Where are you going?'

'None of your business. But don't tell Lizzie I've

gone out, OK? I'll be back before Dad gets home. Is that the letter?'

I nodded.

'Cool.' Before I could stop him, he had snatched it from me, dived into the bathroom and slammed the door.

In my bedroom, I flopped down on my bed feeling fed up. I started to flick through the section in my new detective book entitled 'Tracking Suspects'. It described how you could follow someone (like a murder suspect, for instance) without them knowing. And it suggested that if you wanted to practise, you could start out by tracking your friends. Or your sister or brother . . .

I quickly read through all the tips about tailing somebody. One of the things the book suggested was that you wear soft footwear so that your footsteps wouldn't be heard. I was still wearing my school shoes so I quickly changed out of them and put on my trainers as I heard the toilet flushing and the bathroom door being opened. In my book it said not to follow the person you were tracking too closely and to allow them thirty seconds to walk away before you started following them, so I waited until I heard Matthew going down the stairs, then started to count one-elephant, two-elephant, three-elephant, like that, up to thirty. Then I tiptoed downstairs myself. The television was turned up quite loudly in the living room and Matthew had obviously managed to open and close the front door without Lizzie hearing. Now I just had to do the same.

I got outside safely and hurried down our driveway. I could see Matthew walking quickly down our road – he was almost at the corner now – and I started to follow him. I just hoped he didn't stop because, according to the book, you weren't meant to just stop walking yourself if your suspect stopped otherwise that would look very suspicious – you were meant to dive into a shop doorway or go and stand behind a tree instead. And there weren't any shops or trees on our street.

I followed Matthew to the end of our road, then round the corner, then down another road, and I wasn't really surprised when he eventually turned into Jennifer's street.

I hid behind a lamp-post (which was the only thing near by that resembled a tree) as he rang her front doorbell, and when Jennifer answered the door, she noticed me standing there immediately – unfortunately I'm a lot wider than a lamp-post – and waved to me.

My brother whirled round and nearly had a fit when he saw me.

'Calm down!' I told him, running over Jennifer's front lawn to join them. 'I only followed you to try out my detective skills and you've got to admit they're pretty good. You didn't know I was behind you at all, did you?'

'Come inside, quickly,' Jennifer said.

'*She's* not coming inside!' Matthew barked.

'If you make me go home, I'll tell Lizzie where you are,' I told him swiftly.

He looked like he was about to throttle me, but fortunately Jennifer intervened. 'Just let her come in, Matty. It's OK.' She led us hastily into the living room, where she pulled Matthew down beside her on the sofa and I was left with the lumpy-looking armchair. Jennifer seemed to know already about her dad writing to ours because straight away she asked, 'What did he say in his letter, Matthew?'

'Here.' Matthew pulled the letter out of his pocket and showed it to her.

She read it through quickly, then looked at him apologetically. 'I'm sorry. Was that why your dad was phoning here?'

'Yeah. He figures that speaking to *your* dad is going to sort it all out – like you and me are about five or something.'

Jennifer sighed. 'Dad thinks you're encouraging me to try and find my mum. He's acting really weirdly about it.' She glanced down at the letter again, shaking her head. 'Oh, this is so stupid!' She tossed it on the floor.

I quickly picked it up and put it in my jacket pocket. If Jennifer's father did walk in suddenly, it would be bad enough him finding Matthew and me there, let alone also finding his private letter to our dad.

'Don't get upset, Jen. It's not your fault.' Matthew was putting his arm round her.

'If the two of you want to have a snog, I can go and hang out in Jennifer's room,' I offered, pretty generously, I thought. 'I can try on some of Jennifer's make-up.'

'Don't you dare—' Matthew began, but Jennifer interrupted him.

'It's OK. She can use it if she wants. It's on my dressing table, Esmie.'

'Thanks!' I grinned, jumping up.

'You don't have to—' I heard Matthew start to say as I left the room.

'I told you, it's OK. I don't mind her borrowing my stuff. I think she's sweet.'

I didn't wait to hear Matthew's answer to *that*.

Up in Jennifer's room I found her make-up bag straight away and started by trying on some purple lipstick. Then I reckoned I'd try on some mascara to make my eyelashes look longer. That's when I noticed – in the mirror – Jennifer's orange and pink bag lying on her bed. The bag was unzipped and I could see the folded-up letter she'd shown me the other day inside – the one her mum had sent her when she was little. I couldn't stop myself taking it out of her bag to have another look. I had my magnifying glass in my pocket and this was another piece of written evidence I could examine. In fact, this was very nearly the real thing since it was a letter that had been written by a real missing person.

I started to read it using the magnifying glass, and that's when I noticed that the capital letter 'a's in the letter from Jennifer's mum were written in exactly the same way as the ones in the letter from Jennifer's dad. I pulled her dad's letter out of my pocket and laid it down beside her mum's, to conduct what my detective book called a *side-by-side comparison*. In both letters, the capital 'a's were all written like oversized small 'a's. And that was in addition to the word 'precious' being spelled wrong in Jennifer's mum's letter in the same way that it was spelled wrong in the letter from Jennifer's dad. Both times the writer had put in an extra 's'.

I stared at the two letters for several minutes, because what I was thinking now just didn't make any sense.

I went downstairs to show Jennifer and Matthew what I had discovered and walked in on them snogging on the sofa. How anyone can snog my brother is beyond me, but when I said that to Holly she didn't agree with me. She said that Matthew has lips that are just the right thickness for snogging – unlike Jennifer's, which are a little bit too thin.

'Hey!' I said loudly, which made them instantly jump about a mile apart from each other. 'I want to show you something.' I sat in between them on the sofa since there was now quite a big space there, holding the two letters I had been examining, one in each hand. 'I've discovered something really weird,' I told them. 'Jennifer, I don't think your mum really did send you that letter when you were a baby.'

'What are you talking about?'

'I've examined the handwriting in both these letters,' I said, sounding spookily like Sherlock

Holmes, even if I do say so myself. I gave them to Jennifer to look at – the one her mum was meant to have sent her years ago and the one her dad had only just sent to our house. 'Look at the handwriting! It looks different because one's written in block capitals and the other isn't, but if you look more closely –' I pointed out the identical capital letter 'a's and the identical misspellings of 'precious' – 'they must have both been written by the same person. Which means that the letter you thought was from your mum can't have been from her at all. It must have been written by your dad. Only why would your dad want you to think your mum had sent you a letter if she hadn't?'

Jennifer was staring at me as if I was talking in a foreign language. (I guess Sherlock Holmes got that a lot too.)

'Read them,' I persisted. I handed her the magnifying glass.

Jennifer read both letters, staring at them closely, saying nothing. Matthew was leaning over her shoulder to look too. As he murmured that he saw what I meant, Jennifer suddenly jumped up from the sofa.

'That's *rubbish*! Of course this letter's from my mum!'

'Jennifer, the writing does look really similar—' Matthew began.

'Stop it!' she snapped. 'Stop interfering! You don't know what you're talking about!'

Matthew looked surprised. 'But you were the one who asked us to—'

'I think you'd better go before my dad gets back. Here! Take this with you!' She threw Dad's letter in Matthew's direction, keeping a tight hold on the one from her mother. 'You've got an overactive imagination, Esmie, that's your problem!'

And she practically threw us out of her house.

Matthew was really agitated on the way home, worrying about Jennifer. And I was worried too. Maybe I shouldn't have just blurted it all out like that. Juliette used to say that it wasn't always right to tell the truth if it was hurtful and if nobody had anything to gain by hearing it. But surely Jennifer *did* have something to gain by knowing the truth? Although I could see why she found it hurtful that her mum *hadn't* written her that letter, because it was the only proof she had that her mum loved her.

Matthew unlocked the front door as quietly as he could when we got back. It sounded like Lizzie was on the phone in the living room and we both stopped in the hall to listen. Was she on the phone to Dad, informing him that she had just discovered we were gone?

She wasn't, thank goodness. She was chatting to one of her friends. Matty headed upstairs straight away, but I paused to listen. And what I heard made me instantly forget about Jennifer and that forged letter from her mother.

'Andrew thinks I should tell John,' I heard Lizzie say. 'But I'm not sure I'm up for that just yet . . . No, it can't go on much longer, but John's so stressed at work with this new case that I'm not sure now's the right time to . . . Yes . . . Yes, I know . . . I know I'm not getting any younger . . .'

Suddenly the doorbell rang, making me jump.

I ran up the stairs as Lizzie came out into the hall and opened the front door – it was Dad's breakdown service. I went into my bedroom, feeling dazed. What had Lizzie meant just now? *What* couldn't go on much longer? Was she having an affair with this Andrew person after all, and waiting for Dad to be less stressed at work before she told him?

I looked at the photograph of my mother that sits by my bed. When I was younger I used to talk to her all the time about stuff and imagine that I could hear her replying to me. But since Lizzie had been around, I'd stopped doing that because I was afraid Lizzie would hear me and think that since I still spoke to my real mum, I didn't need her as well. 'Mum, what shall I do?' I asked now. 'What if Lizzie's being unfaithful to Dad? What if she leaves us?'

But, as usual, my mother's picture didn't reply, which is why I really did need Lizzie too.

In no time at all I had thought up a cunning plan (as Sherlock Holmes might say) to find out the truth. I was going to hide in Lizzie's car on Saturday morning and follow her when she went to meet Andrew. I had seen an American TV film recently where the private detective hid in the boot of his suspect's car after shooting bullet holes in it first to make sure he could breathe. Well, there was no way I was climbing into Lizzie's boot, but I reckoned I could easily lie down flat behind the front seats and follow her that way.

Lizzie stayed over at our house on Friday night, so on Saturday morning her car was parked in our driveway beside Dad's. At half-past nine, Lizzie was upstairs getting dressed, Dad was in the kitchen swigging down a quick cup of coffee before he set off for work, and Matthew was still in bed. I took Lizzie's car keys off the hall table, slipped outside and unlocked her car door, then quickly returned the keys before dodging back outside again. I climbed into the back of her car, locked the door again from the inside, and lay down flat on the floor behind the front seats, pulling the travel rug over me. With any luck, when Lizzie got in the car she wouldn't bother looking in the back.

I lay there for five minutes, starting to get uncomfortable. I heard Dad come outside and try to start his car. His breakdown service had done a temporary fixing job when they'd come out to it the other day, but they'd told Dad he needed to take it to a garage to get it sorted properly. Dad hadn't got round to doing that yet and now it sounded like the engine had conked out again. The next thing I knew, Lizzie and Dad were both in the driveway and Lizzie was offering to get the bus into town so that Dad could take her car to work this morning. Before I could get out, Dad was getting in and sliding back the driver's seat, because he's got longer legs than Lizzie, which meant I had to roll over on to my side really quickly so as not to get crushed.

I lay there fuming as Dad drove off because I knew that there was no way I was going to be able to follow Lizzie now – and that I was going to have to be really careful not to be caught by Dad since he's always going on about how important it is not to muck around in cars and to always wear your seat belt.

We had driven all the way to Dad's work and had just pulled up in the car park when his mobile started ringing. 'Hello?' I heard him say. 'Where are you?' He listened for a bit, then asked, 'Did they find anything else at the allotments?'

I instantly pricked up my ears. Dad was talking

about his latest murder case – the one he'd flatly refused to give us any details about when we'd asked.

'What about forensics?' he was saying. 'Well, we knew that much . . . What? OK, so we know it's an adult female skeleton . . . What? . . . A healed fracture to the right arm . . . OK . . . So how are we doing with the dental and hospital records? . . . OK . . . Sure . . . What about missing persons? . . . Right . . . OK . . . Well, keep me posted.'

He put his phone away and got out of the car.

My heart was beating really fast as I waited for him to walk away. The skeleton that had been found in Jennifer's dad's allotments belonged to an adult female who had once broken her arm. Well, I knew of a missing person who had once broken her arm, didn't I? And whose husband did a lot of digging on those allotments . . .

'I suppose it might not have been murder. It could just have been manslaughter,' I pointed out to Holly when I told her everything on the phone as soon as I got back home. I knew from asking Dad ages ago that murder was premeditated whereas manslaughter wasn't. If you committed manslaughter it meant you'd killed somebody on the spur of the moment, rather than actually planned to do it. 'Jennifer's dad's got a really bad temper,' I continued. 'What if he was having a row with Jennifer's mum and he completely lost it? What if he pushed her and she fell and hit her head and died? And then he didn't want anyone to find out what he'd done so he buried her in the allotments.'

'Esmie, that's crazy!'

'No, it's not,' I said defensively. 'It would explain why he acted so weirdly when Jennifer wanted to find her mum. And it would explain why he forged that letter too. If anyone got suspicious about her disappearing, that letter would make it seem like she was still alive.'

'Except that he didn't disguise his handwriting very well,' Holly pointed out.

'Yes, but he didn't think it would be read by a handwriting expert, did he?'

'Like you, you mean?' Holly sounded like she was mocking me. 'Esmie, I think you're getting a bit carried away with all this detective stuff. There could easily be another explanation for those letters being written by the same person, and for Jennifer's dad never wanting to talk about her mum.'

'Like what?' I demanded huffily.

'Well . . .' She sounded quite excited now. 'There was a programme on TV a couple of nights ago about people who've had sex-change operations. I've been thinking . . . What if Jennifer's mum had a sex-change operation and became a man when Jennifer was still a baby? Maybe she didn't know how to explain it to Jennifer so she thought the easiest way was to pretend she was her dad instead?'

'Holly, don't be stupid!' I burst out.

'I'm not being stupid! *I* happen to think it's important for a detective to keep an open mind at all times.' Holly was speaking in her most confident, know-it-all voice, and for a moment I felt as if *she* was Sherlock Holmes and I was only Doctor Watson.

'It's also important for a detective to have good observation skills,' I retaliated. 'And you obviously haven't noticed that Jennifer's father has got really broad shoulders, really big hands and that he's quite hairy. And that makes it *very* unlikely that he was a woman.'

'That could be because of hormone therapy,' Holly said promptly. 'I read all about that in one of Mum's magazines.'

Fortunately, the doorbell rang at that point and I told her I had to go. I nearly wet myself when I looked through the window to see who it was though. It was Mr Mitchell, looking very big and very unshaven, so either he was definitely a man or he'd had an awful lot of hormone therapy. Dad still hadn't got to speak to him on the phone because, whenever he'd tried to, Mr Mitchell had been out – or at least he had been according to Jennifer, who had answered the phone each time he'd rung. I could only guess that Mr Mitchell had decided to come round to speak to Dad in person.

I was all alone in the house. When I'd got back from my secret trip in Lizzie's car, followed by the bus ride home again, I'd found our house completely empty and I'd only been able to get in because I'd got my key with me. I knew where Dad and Lizzie were, of course, but Matthew had told Dad that he would stay at home with me that morning so I had expected him to be there when I got back.

There was no way I was opening the door to Mr Mitchell now.

He rang the bell a few more times, then turned and left.

I was making myself a drink in the kitchen a few minutes later, when I heard a banging on the back door and Matthew's voice calling, 'Esmie? Are you in there?'

I opened the door straight away. Matthew and Jennifer were standing there. Jennifer was holding a big blue holdall. 'Jennifer, your dad was just here—' I began.

'We know,' Matthew interrupted me. 'That's why we came round the back. Jennifer's run away and she's going to stay here for a bit.'

'Run away?' I gasped, staring at Jennifer. 'Why? I mean . . . did he do something to you?' I was imagining Jennifer's dad losing his temper and pushing *her* now – or worse.

'I'm so sorry for the way I acted the other day, Esmie,' Jennifer said. 'I couldn't stop thinking about those letters after you'd gone, and last night I asked Dad about that letter from my mum and the thing is . . . he admitted that he *did* write it!'

I stared at her, too stunned to speak. Whatever I'd expected her to say, it wasn't that.

'Dad says he thought it would make me feel better when I got older if I had a nice letter from my mother saying that she hadn't *wanted* to leave me behind and that I was really precious to her and everything. So he wrote that letter and pretended it was from her.'

I was still silent. I mean, what could you say in answer to that? I certainly couldn't just blurt out that I was pretty certain he was lying and that his real reason for forging that letter had been much more sinister.

'Anyway, when he told me that, I decided I didn't want to contact her after all – not right now, anyway – so I phoned Matty this morning to ask him to email that Internet missing-persons agency again and tell them to forget it.' She looked at my brother. 'And I also wanted to tell him I was sorry about what I said before. Well, Dad heard me on the phone and went ballistic! We had a terrible row. I told him I was going to carry on seeing Matthew whether he liked it or not. He said I was grounded and I wasn't allowed out of the house. So I phoned Matthew from my mobile afterwards and told him I was running away.'

'I went to meet her at the bottom of her road,'

Matthew explained. 'I couldn't find you anywhere in the house to tell you. Where were you, Esmie?'

'I just popped out for a few minutes,' I mumbled. Then, to stop him asking any more questions, I added quickly. 'Do you really think Dad'll let Jennifer move in with us?'

'Jennifer's sixteen, so she's legally allowed to choose where she wants to live, so it should be cool.'

'You reckon?' I could almost hear Dad pointing out in his most sarcastic voice that since *he* was also over sixteen, *he* was legally allowed to choose who it would be cool to have living in his house with him.

'He won't kick her out once he's heard how horrible her dad was to her,' Matthew added.

'Why? What did he do?'

'It's what he said!' Jennifer answered. 'Really nasty things. He really scared me. He said he'd skin Matthew alive if he caught him with me again and he yelled all this horrible stuff at me, about how I was just like my mother . . .' She sniffed.

'Your *mother*?' I couldn't think about Jennifer's mother now without thinking about that skeleton with the broken arm. 'I guess your dad didn't like your mum very much, huh?'

'Not after she walked out on him – no!'

'What about before that?' I was trying to sound

casual, though really I had slipped into full detective mode. 'Did they row a lot?'

'Shut it, Esmie.' Matthew glared at me like he thought I was being really insensitive. 'Lizzie'll be back soon,' he grunted, glancing at the kitchen clock. 'We won't say anything about Jennifer staying until Dad gets back. I'll tell him when he's had something to eat and a glass of wine and he's in a good mood. *I'll* tell him, Esmie, OK? I don't want you opening your big mouth and doing it!'

'OK! OK!' I grumbled. Though I don't reckon I've got a big mouth at all.

We were upstairs settling Jennifer into Juliette's old room when the doorbell rang again. We knew it couldn't be Dad or Lizzie because they both had keys.

'Let's just leave it,' Matthew said as he headed through to Dad's room to get some spare sheets out of the airing cupboard.

'Esmie, do you think your dad'll be angry because Matthew's invited me to stay?' Jennifer asked me after he'd gone.

'Probably,' I answered. 'But don't worry – his bark's worse than his bite. He'll calm down after he's yelled for a bit.'

'Unlike *my* Dad then.'

'How do you mean?' I asked, having a sudden

vision of Jennifer's father sporting enormous white fangs and swooping down on Jennifer's mother to bite her in the jugular vein. And of course a bite mark wouldn't show up on a skeleton. I quickly told myself I had to get a grip. After all, this was real life, not an episode of *Buffy the Vampire Slayer*.

'It's just that my dad isn't a very calm person,' Jennifer answered.

'You know, I wouldn't worry so much about your dad, Jen . . .' Matthew was saying as he came back into the room carrying some folded sheets and pillowcases. 'Dads are all the same! You know when yours started ranting on about how he'd skin me alive if he caught me inside his house again? Well, that's the sort of thing my dad comes out with all the time. They're all mouth about what they're going to do to you. They don't mean any of it!'

'Maybe Jennifer's dad really *would* skin you alive,' I muttered under my breath. After all, there was still that skeleton in the allotments to think about. I didn't see how you could tell whether a skeleton's skin was absent because it had rotted away naturally or for some other reason.

My comment was drowned out by the doorbell ringing again – and this time it kept on ringing.

'What if it's Dad?' Jennifer suddenly looked scared. 'What if he's found out I'm here?'

'Someone had better answer the door,' Matthew said, looking at me. 'Go on, Esmie. If it's Jennifer's dad, just tell him you don't know where we are.'

'*I'm* not answering the door to him!'

'It's OK, Esmie,' Jennifer said. 'He's not mad at *you*.'

'Yes, but . . .' How could I tell them why I was just as scared of Jennifer's father as they were? Just then the ringing stopped and we heard heavy footsteps on the gravel path that runs round the side of the house.

'Did you lock the back door?' Matthew asked me.

'Why? Didn't *you* lock it?'

Matthew looked at Jennifer in alarm and I could tell he couldn't remember whether he had or not.

'Maybe I'd better just go down and speak to him,' Jennifer said anxiously. 'Before he gets even angrier.'

'NO!' I shrieked. 'Come on! We've all got to lock ourselves in the bathroom!'

Matthew and Jennifer clearly thought I was taking this a bit too far. 'Esmie, he's not going to *murder* us,' my brother said impatiently.

And that was too much for me. 'You don't know that!' I screeched. 'I heard Dad talking on the phone about that body they found. It sounds like Jennifer's mum!'

Jennifer's eyes immediately turned into saucers and she just gaped at me. So did Matthew.

Suddenly we heard the front door opening and Lizzie's voice.

'Lizzie!' I yelled, running downstairs. And before I realized what was happening, I was running headlong into Jennifer's dad as he stepped in through the door in front of her.

I screamed. He jumped. Lizzie started asking what was the matter. I think I might have screamed again but I'm not sure. Lizzie hurriedly ushered Mr Mitchell into the living room as I ran into the kitchen and started looking for a weapon I could use in self-defence. 'You've got to make him leave!' I burst out as Lizzie joined me. 'Please, Lizzie . . .' I went and picked up our heaviest frying pan.

I don't know what went through Lizzie's mind at that point, but she looked very worried and quickly left me again to go and speak to Mr Mitchell. 'I'm sorry but I'm going to have to ask you to leave at once, please,' I heard her say. 'I don't know where your daughter is, but I do know that Esmie is very upset about something. I don't know what's wrong with her, but I need you to go so that I can find out.'

In the kitchen I held my breath, half-expecting him to refuse, but that didn't happen. He said something in a quiet voice and Lizzie said something back and then she was showing him out.

She came straight into the kitchen afterwards. 'Esmie, what is it? What's wrong? Where's Matthew?'

Where *was* Matthew? And why hadn't he come downstairs to help me? Maybe he had decided to stay with Jennifer to protect *her*.

'He's upstairs,' I gasped, lowering the frying pan.

'Why are you so frightened?'

I didn't answer. I was still trembling.

She stared at me for a moment or two, then frowned. 'Esmie, come through to the living room with me and we'll sit down and talk about it, OK?' She put her arm round me as we walked through to the other room. I noticed that she shut the living-room door behind us as if she thought I might want to keep whatever I had to say private. 'I don't want you to be afraid to tell me anything, Esmie,' she said gently as she sat down beside me on the sofa. She paused. 'Has Jennifer's father ever done anything to hurt you – or upset you – in any way?'

I bit my lip. Should I tell her or shouldn't I? I had told Holly and she hadn't taken me seriously. What if Lizzie didn't believe me either?

Lizzie's forehead was all bunched up. 'Tell me,

Esmie – whatever it is. I promise I'll try and help. Just tell me, please . . .'

And that's when I decided to trust her. 'I think that maybe . . . that maybe he might have . . .' I sniffed. 'I think he might have . . . *killed* Jennifer's mum!'

Lizzie gaped at me. She looked completely gob-smacked. 'Esmie, what are you talking about?'

'It might not have been on purpose,' I added quickly. I told her how Jennifer's dad had a really bad temper, and my theory about it being manslaughter rather than murder. I also told her about our hunt for Jennifer's mother and how Jennifer's dad had been so much against it. And I told her how Jennifer's father had written a fake letter to Jennifer, pretending it was from her mum, and how I didn't believe his explanation for that, though Jennifer seemed to. And lastly, I mentioned that Jennifer's mum had broken her arm when she was pregnant. 'And you know that dead body Dad's investigating – the one they found on Jennifer's dad's allotments? Well, *it's* got a broken arm too!'

Lizzie listened to all of this, looking incredulous. When I got to the end, she asked, 'How do you know it's got a broken arm?'

I flushed. How could I tell her that I'd overheard Dad talking when I'd been hiding in her car, trying to spy on her? 'Dad told me,' I mumbled.

'Really?' I could tell she found that hard to believe. She stayed silent for a few moments. I thought I heard a noise in the hall and I was about to ask Lizzie to check that the front door was still locked, when she said, 'Esmie, have you told any of this to your father?'

I shook my head.

'Well, I think you'd better. Esmie, there are lots of missing people out there. And lots of people with broken arms. So I really don't think you should mention any of this to Matthew in case he says something to Jennifer which might—' She stopped abruptly as she saw the look on my face. 'You haven't already said something?'

I coloured even more. 'Only just now when we were upstairs. I thought Jennifer's dad was break-ing in. I had to tell them he was dangerous so they'd hide from him.'

'*Them?*'

'Jennifer's upstairs too.'

Lizzie looked like she was trying very hard to get all this straight in her mind. 'And you just told her . . . just now . . . that you think her dad might have murdered her mum?'

'Well, I didn't . . . e-exactly . . . say *that*,' I stammered. Now that I was hearing Lizzie say it, I had to admit that it didn't sound like the smartest thing to have just blurted out, especially as I was pretty sure that I hadn't actually used the words, *might have*.

'Come with me,' Lizzie said, standing up. 'Matthew! Jennifer!' she called out when we reached the stairs, but there was no reply.

Jennifer's holdall was gone from the spare room and a note addressed to Dad had been left on Matthew's bed.

'Do you think they've *both* run away now?' I asked in disbelief.

'I hope not,' Lizzie said, but she was looking very worried as she picked up the note and started to unfold it.

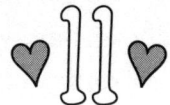

You'd think that since Dad is a detective and used to having missing persons reported to him, he'd be cooler than most people when Lizzie phoned him up and told him about Matthew – especially as Matthew had only been missing for about ten minutes. But he wasn't.

He left his murder investigation and came straight home, and from the time he stepped in through our front door all he did was panic. It was Lizzie who was the sensible one.

'They can't have gone far,' she kept saying. 'They've probably just gone to stay with a friend. I expect they'll phone us soon – or even come home.'

'Let me see that note again,' Dad grunted. But all Matthew's note said was that he and Jennifer were going away for a while and not to worry about them.

Dad phoned Matthew's mobile of course, but it was switched off. He left a pretty ranty message on it at first, then after he'd had time to get less angry and more worried, he phoned back and left a calmer one. In between his two calls to Matthew, he phoned Jennifer's dad, but Mr Mitchell wasn't in.

In among all this phoning, Lizzie suggested I had better tell Dad everything that had been happening, so I had to tell him about Jennifer rowing with her dad and running away, and how Matthew had said she could stay here with us.

'So why did they need to run off again?' Dad asked.

I flushed and said nothing.

'Esmie mentioned something to Jennifer that might have got her a bit upset,' Lizzie explained gently. 'Tell him, Esmie.'

I took a deep breath. 'I told her about the body in the allotments maybe being her mother.'

'You told her *what*?' Dad looked flabbergasted.

I told him about Jennifer's mum having a broken arm. 'Just like your skeleton, Dad,' I pointed out.

'How do you know about that? We haven't released that information to anybody yet!'

'Haven't you?' I gasped. 'Don't you think you should? It might help jog the memories of the general public – like on *Crimewatch*!'

'Thanks for the tip.' He was glaring at me. 'Now, answer my question.'

I quickly tried to think up a way of telling him the truth, without telling him everything. 'I overheard you talking about it on the phone,' I began. 'I didn't mean to. I wasn't listening on purpose. I . . . er . . . well, I was in the car.'

'The *car*?'

'I was hiding behind the seats when you borrowed Lizzie's car this morning. You see, it was meant to be a . . . a . . . joke,' I continued rapidly. 'I was going to jump up and surprise Lizzie, you see – but then you got in the car and I thought I'd wait a bit, and then . . . and then I decided not to because I knew you'd be angry.'

Dad looked angry then all right, and started going on about how I was too old to be playing jokes like that. He said it was stupid and dangerous to hide in a car, not wearing a seat belt, and what if there'd been an accident?

'I know, Dad,' I said quickly. 'I'm sorry. But are you going to take Mr Mitchell in for questioning now or what?'

All of a sudden, Dad got this strange, dark look on his face. 'Esmie, don't you think you've done enough harm already, opening your mouth and blurting out all that rubbish to Jennifer?'

'But it isn't rubbish!' I protested.

'Isn't it? Esmie, you've terrified her so much that she doesn't even feel it's safe to stay *here*.'

'I know, but . . .' My voice dried up. I couldn't remember Dad ever looking at me as coldly as he was looking at me now.

'Just go to your room where you can't cause any more trouble. Go on!'

I felt a lump in my throat and tears pricking my eyes. My legs felt wobbly. I stumbled up to my bedroom and burst into tears. It wasn't fair! How could Dad say I was talking rubbish when, for all he knew, that skeleton *could* be Jennifer's mum? And if it was, then that made Mr Mitchell a prime suspect, didn't it? Dad was always saying that most murder victims were killed by someone they knew – and Mrs Mitchell had certainly known Mr Mitchell, hadn't she? OK, so I had upset Jennifer with what I'd said, but I'd only been trying to keep her safe. It wasn't my fault that she'd run away and taken my brother with her!

Whenever I cry, my nose always starts running. I reached for a tissue from the box by my bed and my hand touched my mother's photograph.

'*You* don't think I'm talking rubbish, do you, Mum?' I murmured. I picked up the photograph and hugged it close to me. When I was younger, I'd really thought of that photo as being *her* and, if I'd had a problem, then seeing her face smiling reassuringly at me and imagining her voice telling me that everything was going to be OK had always been enough to make me feel better. But it wasn't making me feel better now.

The front door slammed and, when I looked out of my bedroom window, I saw Dad getting into Lizzie's car. I guessed he had decided to go out and look for Matthew and Jennifer himself.

I heard Lizzie coming upstairs so I quickly put down my mother's photograph because, like I said before, I'm always very careful to give Lizzie the impression that I don't give my real mother too much thought at all.

'Esmie?' Lizzie knocked on my door and came into my room. 'Your dad's just gone to speak to Mr Mitchell.'

'*What?* On his own?' Policemen weren't meant to go and confront murderers on their own. Everyone knew that. They were meant to take back-up with them.

'He's just gone to tell him about Matthew and Jennifer. Then he's going to Jake's to see if they've gone there – or if Jake knows where they could be.'

'Dad doesn't believe me about Jennifer's dad being dangerous, does he?' I said, scowling.

'Esmie, I think you should let your dad worry about that since he's the one in charge of the investigation, not you,' Lizzie said lightly. 'Right now, I think we should be trying to come up with ideas about where Matthew and Jennifer might have gone.' She paused. 'Could they have gone looking for Jennifer's mother, do you think?'

'What? In the police mortuary?' I knew that the police kept any dead bodies they found in the mortuary and I assumed they did the same with any suspicious skeletons.

'*Esmie* . . .' Lizzie looked at me like she thought I was deliberately being awkward.

'Well, Dad thinks Jennifer believed me about her mum!' I said, hearing my voice rising several notes higher than usual. '*He* thinks she believed what I said and that's why she ran away! *He* thinks this is all my fault!'

'Of course he doesn't think that,' Lizzie protested. 'He's just very worried. It made him lose his temper quicker than normal, that's all.'

'I mean it's not like we don't know Matty's safe,' I pointed out huffily. 'He left a note to tell us he's run away. So we know he's not missing because he's been kidnapped or anything.'

'Yes, but it's not quite that simple, Esmie. It's what might happen to him *now* that your dad's worried about. Matty may seem quite grown up to you, but he's still your dad's child.'

'Dad's overprotective,' I grunted. Matty is always saying that, and I reckon he's right.

'Well, I expect I'd be overprotective too, if I'd had to bring up two children on my own,' Lizzie was saying. 'It must be very hard not having another parent to share your worries with. And the job he does can't help. He knows far more than most people about all the dangers that are out there.'

'So *you* think he's overprotective too!' I burst out. 'Good! As soon as he gets home, I'm going to tell him that!'

Lizzie looked annoyed. 'Maybe that's not such a great idea, eh, Esmie?' she said quite sharply. 'Considering what's happened today.'

'Well, it isn't fair of him to take it out on me, just because he's worried,' I protested. 'I mean, I didn't *make* Matthew run away, did I?' I felt tears pricking my eyes again.

'Esmie, I told you! Your dad *doesn't* blame you!' She sounded like she was losing patience with me now.

'Yes he does.' I glanced at my mother's photo. 'I bet he doesn't even think *she'd* be proud of me any more.' I picked up the photograph, not caring now that Lizzie was watching me. Something that Dad had always told me, right from when I was little, was that if my mother was still alive she'd be really proud of how I'd turned out.

'Oh, Esmie . . . Of course your dad hasn't changed his mind about that!' Lizzie said. 'There's a lot for her to be proud of!'

I nearly asked, *Like what?* But instead I heard myself asking in my most pathetic voice, 'Would *you* still feel proud of me if *you* were her?'

'Of course I would!'

I nearly asked her then if she wished she *was* my mother, but I was too scared to, in case she didn't give me the answer I wanted, because she wasn't looking all that maternal right now. She was looking pretty harassed.

Matthew didn't call for the whole of that day, or the next, and by Monday morning Dad was looking really tired from hardly getting any sleep over the weekend. I reckoned Lizzie must have spoken to him about me because he came into my bedroom on Saturday night and told me that he certainly didn't blame me for my brother running away. But he also mentioned again how wrong it had been to hide like that in the back of his car and listen in to his private phone call. And he said that he wished I would go straight to him in future, if I ever got any ideas in my head about any of the people we knew being murderers.

The other thing he told me was that he'd spoken to Jennifer's dad and satisfied himself that his story about Mrs Mitchell leaving when Jennifer was little was true. Besides, he added, they were fairly sure now about the identity of that skeleton. He wouldn't tell me anything else, but he said that all would be revealed in due course and that I'd certainly got it wrong about the skeleton being Jennifer's mother.

I know I should have been relieved when he said that, and I was – because it was obviously much better for Jennifer if her father *wasn't* a murderer – but I couldn't help feeling a little bit disappointed at the same time. I guess Sherlock Holmes probably felt a bit discouraged too whenever *he* discovered that he'd got one of his cases completely wrong.

On Monday at school, I told Holly everything that had happened. She said she'd known all along that the skeleton wasn't Jennifer's mother. Then she started comparing Matthew to various cool characters who had run away in different films she'd seen, until I got really fed up with listening to her. My brother's disappearing act just couldn't be compared with Steve McQueen's heroic attempt to escape from a German prisoner-of-war camp in *The Great Escape*, as far as I was concerned. Later, as we were sitting next to each other in French, she came up with the idea that Matthew and Jennifer had run away to Scotland to get married. She said she'd seen a TV programme about a teenage couple who'd done that. Apparently, you can get married in Scotland when you're sixteen without your parents' permission, whereas in England you can't.

I was still thinking about that when I got home that afternoon and, as soon as I walked in through our front door, I knew something had happened. Dad was home early and he was talking on the phone to somebody. It didn't take me long to work out that the person he was talking to was Jennifer's father.

'Of course I'm not happy about it, but at least we know they're OK,' Dad was saying a bit impatiently.

I rushed over, afraid that I already knew what it was that he was unhappy about. 'Have Matty and Jennifer gone to Scotland to get married?' I asked breathlessly.

Dad stopped his conversation with Mr Mitchell in mid-sentence and stared at me. 'Have they *told* you they want to get married?'

I shook my head. 'No. It was just something Holly saw on TV. But—'

He held up his hand to stop me, then quickly lifted the phone back to his ear and spent several minutes calming down Mr Mitchell (who had over-heard the word 'married' and was now freaking out big time).

After he came off the phone, Dad told me that Matthew had left a message on our answering machine that afternoon. 'He says they're both fine, that they've got somewhere to stay . . . though he doesn't say where . . . and that he'll ring again in a few days . . . No doubt he'll pick some other time when he knows I'll be out . . .' Dad had walked over to the window as he was talking, and now he was staring out of it as if he was searching for my brother. 'I'm telling you, Esmie . . . When I get my hands on that boy . . .'

The phone started ringing before he could finish and, as I was nearer, I got to it before Dad could. 'Hello?'

'May I speak to Esmerelda Harvey, please?'

'This is Esmie,' I replied, puzzled because nobody I knew called me Esmerelda. Dad was mouthing Matthew's name at me and I shook my head to let him know that it wasn't my brother.

'This is Helen Forbes. You sent me a letter recently.'

'Oh!' What with everything else that had happened, I'd completely forgotten about writing to those two lady doctors to try and find Jennifer's aunt. I couldn't think what to say. 'Are you . . . ? I mean, do you . . . ?' I trailed off.

'I think,' the voice continued, pausing slightly, 'that your friend, Jennifer, may be my niece.'

Dad was still standing watching me, wondering who it was on the phone. I didn't know what to do. Should I tell Dad who was calling? But I hadn't told anyone else about my letter to Jennifer's aunt – except Holly, of course. I hadn't even told Jennifer or Matthew. If I told Dad then I knew he would take over immediately. He would probably phone Jennifer's dad and tell *him*.

'It's a bit difficult for me to talk right now,' I said into the mouthpiece. 'Can I take your number and call you back? Or *she* will.' I didn't want to say Jennifer's name while Dad was in the room.

'Why didn't Jennifer contact me herself if she wanted to find out about her mother?' the woman asked.

'Er . . . she . . . well . . . sh-she thought it was best if you phoned me to start with,' I stammered.

There was a pause. 'Does her father *know* she's contacted me?'

I swallowed, remembering how Juliette had said that it wasn't always necessary – or wise – to tell the truth about certain things. I knew that if I told the truth here, I could be making problems for Jennifer, since her aunt might be the type of adult who would want everything to be out in the open, with all the grown-ups agreeing, before she gave away any information about her sister. 'She's been waiting to see if you phoned back first,' I mumbled.

There was a pause at the other end. 'Well, tell her that she *must* tell her father before she phones me. I mean that. I'll give you my number.'

'I'll get a pen.' Before I could start looking around for one, Dad produced his own pen and notepad from his jacket pocket. He was watching quite closely as I wrote down Jennifer's aunt's number, so I covered my writing with my other hand like I do when anyone's trying to copy my work at school. As soon as I'd put down the phone, I ripped out the page with the number on and put it in my pocket, then I ripped out the three blank pages *under* that page and put them in my pocket too before I gave his notebook back to him. (In my detective book it says how it's possible to read the *indentations* left on a notepad after writing on and removing the top sheet.)

Dad watched the destruction of his notepad with

a half-amused look on his face. Then he demanded to know who I'd been talking to.

I had to think fast. 'It was a girl at school phoning with a message for Holly.'

'Why doesn't she phone Holly directly?'

'She doesn't have Holly's number. Holly doesn't want her to have it,' I added quickly. 'They sort of fell out about something. I can't really tell you any more.'

Dad rolled his eyes as if he thought that me acting as a sort of personal secretary for Holly was really silly, but he didn't say anything else. As soon as he'd gone back into the kitchen, I went upstairs to use the phone in his bedroom where I wouldn't be overheard. I quickly rang Matty's mobile number. All I got was the voicemail thing so I left a message on it. 'Matty, this is Esmie. Tell Jennifer I've managed to contact her mum's sister – her Aunt Helen. I wrote her a letter and she just phoned me and gave me her number for Jennifer to phone her back. I think she might know where Jennifer's mum is. Oh . . . and listen . . . I made a mistake about that skeleton . . . Dad says there's no way it could be Jennifer's mother . . . I'm really sorry I said that . . .' I heard Dad coming up the stairs so I quickly said goodbye and hung up.

I was leaving Dad's bedroom as he reached the landing. 'What are you doing in there?'

'Nothing.' I flushed. 'I was looking for my . . . my *Mizz* magazine. I thought maybe Lizzie had borrowed it.' It was scary how good at lying I was getting these days.

'Well, you can ask her later. She's coming round to babysit at six o'clock while I go back to work for a couple of hours.'

'*Babysit?*' I scowled at him. Dad knows how I feel about him using that word.

'Sorry . . . *Child*mind.' He went into the bathroom and shut the door.

I went into my bedroom to make a start on my homework. I had just opened my maths book – and closed it again because I hate maths – when the phone started ringing. Dad was coming out of the bathroom by then and I heard him go into his bedroom to answer it.

I jumped up and went to join him.

'Hello?' he was saying. But whoever it was didn't speak to him. 'Probably a wrong number,' Dad grunted as he put down the phone, but I could tell he also had another thought about who the caller might have been.

I was certain I knew. I had only just left that message on Matty's mobile. He had probably listened to it by now and was desperate to speak to me about it. He had probably been hoping that I would pick up the phone instead of Dad.

I got on with my homework until Lizzie arrived just after six. I ran downstairs to greet her and noticed that Dad didn't give her a kiss like he normally did when he opened the door to her. He just launched straight into telling her about the message Matty had left on our answering machine this afternoon.

After Dad had spent the next half-hour talking to Lizzie about Matthew, he looked at his watch and said he really did have to go back to work for a couple of hours, even though he didn't much feel like it. He told Lizzie the garage had said his car couldn't be fixed until the new part they had ordered for it arrived. She said he could carry on using her car in the meantime as it was easy enough for her to catch the bus to work, and it was then that he gave her a kiss – a bit belatedly, I thought.

After Dad had gone, Lizzie made me a snack for tea, which I told her I'd take upstairs to eat while I finished my homework. What I really wanted to do was sneak into Dad's bedroom and use the phone in there to call Matthew again. I reckoned his mobile would still be switched off, but maybe if I left him a message letting him know that Dad was out, then he'd ring me back straight away.

I sat down on Dad's bed, lifted the receiver and

was about to start dialling when I realized that Lizzie was on the line downstairs.

'Thanks, Andrew,' she was saying. 'It's just that I *really* need to see you. I don't think I can wait until Saturday.' She sounded stressed.

I froze as a well-spoken male voice answered her. 'How about tomorrow? I'm out at a meeting in the afternoon but I should be back by five. Can you get here OK?'

'John's still using my car but that's no problem. I'll leave work early and catch the bus.'

'Great! See you then, Lizzie!'

I felt sick after she'd hung up. Because how could she and this Andrew person just be friends if she needed to see him as badly as that?

'Dad always called *his* girlfriend on his mobile when he was having *his* affair,' Holly said when I phoned her up straight afterwards and repeated the conversation I had overheard to her. 'It's really stupid of Lizzie to use the landline, see, because your dad'll see the call when he gets his phone bill.' Holly was making it sound like the main point here was that *her* family were experts at having affairs whereas mine were rubbish at it.

'But do you think Lizzie really *is* . . . y-you know . . .' I stammered, not even able to bring myself to say the words.

'Being unfaithful to your dad?' Holly finished for me. 'Well, it kind of looks like it, doesn't it?'

'You don't think there could be some other explanation?'

'Come on, Esmie.' She started to speak in her most solemn, junior-therapist-type voice. 'You're obviously in denial about this. I mean, it's understandable that you want to pretend it isn't happening, but that's only going to make things worse in the end. The thing is, when is Lizzie going to tell him? Because if she doesn't tell him soon, then maybe *you* should!'

'I know, but . . .' How could I explain how I felt about actually telling Dad – as if *telling* him would somehow make it real.

'Somebody's got to tell him. Unless . . .' She paused. 'Do you want me to ask my mum if *she'll* tell him? After all, she *is* training to be a professional counsellor. Not that she'd charge him anything, of course.'

'No thanks!' I replied quickly. Like I said before, Dad thinks therapists and analysts belong in Hollywood movies – preferably *funny* movies – rather than in real life.

There was a long pause, which I knew meant that Holly was giving this a lot of thought. 'You know that detective kit you've got?' she finally asked. 'Does it have any suggestions for *disguises* in it?'

'How do you mean?'

'Well, I reckon the best thing to do to make absolutely *sure* that Lizzie is having an affair before you tell your dad, is to follow her and see where she goes at five o'clock tomorrow. But since Lizzie knows what you look like, you'll need to use some sort of disguise to avoid her seeing you.'

'Like *what*?'

'Well . . . my mum's got this long blonde wig she used to wear to fancy-dress parties. You could use that. Or you could make your face all dark with make-up and wear a sari and then you'd look Indian. I bet Soraya would lend you a sari if we asked her.'

'Soraya never wears saris.' Soraya sits behind us in French and, although her parents come from India, she's lived in England all her life.

'Not to *school*, but I bet she's got one for special occasions. Or the other thing you could do is dress up as a boy!' Holly was beginning to sound quite excited. 'That should be easy enough if we tuck your hair up so it doesn't show. Or you could dress up as a football supporter! You can ask Billy Sanderson if you can borrow his Arsenal gear. He fancies you so he's bound to say yes.'

139

'He does not fancy me!' I protested. 'And I'm definitely not wearing anything of *his*!'

'OK, well, how about I bring my mum's wig to school tomorrow and you can try it on? I can borrow my granny's spare glasses too, if you like. Mum and I are going round to see her tonight. Mind you, she's got very thick lenses so I'm not sure if you'll be able to actually *see* through them.' She suddenly giggled. 'I can see why your dad likes being a detective. It's fun!'

I nearly told her sharply that Dad doesn't dress up in blonde wigs and saris and other people's glasses to track down *his* suspects, but I decided I'd better end the phone call there because I still hadn't called Matty again.

I left my brother a quick message letting him know that Dad was out. Then, just after I'd put down the phone and settled down to wait for him to phone back, Dad arrived home. I couldn't believe it. Normally when Dad says he's going back into work for a couple of hours, he means at least four.

'That didn't take long,' I heard Lizzie say to him in the hall. She sounded surprised to see him back so soon as well.

'I really needed to catch up on some paperwork but I just couldn't concentrate on it. I can't seem to keep my mind on anything at the moment.'

'Well, what do you expect, John?' Lizzie spoke in a very soft voice. 'You're worried sick about Matthew. It's understandable.'

'I'm telling you, Lizzie, I haven't felt this worried since . . .' His voice cracked and, by the time I joined them in the hall, Lizzie was giving him a hug.

I stared at them. If Lizzie *was* having an affair – which I still couldn't quite believe she *was*, despite all the evidence against her – then she was the best actress ever. But the thing that upset me most was how tired and stressed Dad looked. I wanted to kill Matthew for doing this to him. If Lizzie was doing what I thought she was doing, then I wanted to kill her even more, but I couldn't be sure about that yet – not until five o'clock tomorrow.

And that's when the phone started ringing.

While Dad was still hugging Lizzie, I rushed past them and picked up the phone in the living room. 'Hi!' I gasped.

'Esmie? It's Matty.'

I nearly yelled out his name, but I stopped myself just in time. Dad was in the doorway now, looking at me. 'It's Holly, Dad,' I called out to him loudly.

'I thought you said he was out?' Matthew grunted in my ear.

'Dad's just got back, Holly,' I said into the phone. 'I can't talk for very long.'

Dad turned and went back to join Lizzie, who had remained in the hall. I waited until I heard them go into the kitchen together before hissing, '*Matthew, where are you?*'

'Never mind that. How did you find Jennifer's aunt?'

'I'll tell you later. She didn't say if she knew where Jennifer's mother is or anything, but she gave me her number and she wants Jennifer to call her. But, Matthew, listen . . . Dad's really worried about you. When are you coming home?'

'Hang on a minute.' In the background, I could hear Matthew relaying what I'd said to Jennifer – minus the part about Dad being really worried.

Then Jennifer came on the phone herself. She sounded excited. 'Esmie, did you really speak to my aunt? What did she say?'

'Just what I told Matthew. Jennifer, you've got to come home. Dad's going crazy worrying about you both, and *your* dad's really upset too. I think you should—'

'Esmie, can you give me the phone number for my aunt?' Jennifer interrupted me. 'Have you got it there?'

'I thought you didn't *want* to find your mum any more.'

'I know, but if my aunt's actually *spoken* to you . . . Can you give me her number quickly, Esmie?

Matthew's phone's about to run out of juice, so we haven't got much time.'

'Well, you'll have to wait, cos it's upstairs . . .' I had put down the phone and got as far as the door when I stopped myself. If I gave them the number now, they might phone Jennifer's aunt from wherever they were and go and visit her. Then they might find out where Jennifer's mother was and go and visit *her*. And then who knew how long it would be before they came back home? Whereas if I *didn't* give them the number . . .

I went back to the telephone and picked it up again. 'Jennifer?'

'That was quick. Matthew's just getting me a pen.'

'Jennifer, I need to speak to him.'

'OK. Give me the number and—'

'No, Jennifer. I want to speak to Matty *now*.'

There was a bit of a silence at the other end, then the sound of Jennifer muttering something, then my brother came on the phone. '*What?*' he barked at me.

The way he said it really annoyed me. 'I'll tell you *what*, Matthew,' I snapped back. 'We're all really worried because we don't know where you are, right? Dad can't even do his work, he's so worried. And *I* think you should come home. So you can tell Jennifer I'm not giving her this number until you and she come back. And if you don't come back, then I'm giving it to her dad instead. Or . . . or maybe I'll just tear it up and then she'll never find her mum!' And I slammed down the phone.

I felt a bit trembly after I'd done it. I felt like I'd overacted or over*re*acted or something. But the more deep breaths I took and the more I thought about it, the more confident I felt that I'd done the right thing.

Lizzie stayed over that night and I kept out of her way by pretending I had lots of homework I had to get on with. I didn't look up when she put her head round the door at eight o'clock to ask if I wanted a drink or anything. I just grunted and carried on reading my book. When Dad came up later to tell me it was time to go to bed, he asked me if I was cross with Lizzie or him about something.

I shook my head. I wanted to tell him that I wasn't at all angry with him but that I was *furious* with Lizzie, but I knew I had to collect my evidence first, like a proper detective, or Dad just wouldn't believe me.

I felt really sorry for Dad because he looked so worn out. And once he found out about Lizzie he was going to feel even worse.

'Don't worry about Matthew, Dad,' I said. 'I'm sure he's fine. And I reckon he'll be home really soon.'

Dad frowned. 'I hope so, Esmie.'

'Anyway, he's sixteen. He can look after himself. He's practically a grown-up.'

'He won't feel very grown up by the time *I've* finished with him,' Dad replied. '*Sixteen!* What does he think he's playing at?' He said it like my brother was still a little kid as far as he was concerned.

'What are you going to do to him when he gets back, Dad?' I asked, suddenly feeling a bit worried that I was luring my brother home to certain death.

'I don't know, Esmie. Right now, all I'm thinking about is how much I *want* him back – and how much I wish he hadn't got together with Jennifer Mitchell. Do you know, I'm starting to think Jennifer's father was right? I reckon that pair *are* a bad influence on each other.'

'But you won't try and stop them seeing each other when they come home, will you?' I asked quickly.

'Somehow I don't think that would be a very successful strategy, do you? Now, come on. Bed.'

'Dad, I'd like to go and see Lizzie at the shop after school tomorrow. I thought I could get the bus into town straight from school and go and surprise her. Is that OK?'

Dad nodded. 'I suppose it's better than you coming home to an empty house.'

'Good. So don't tell her or it won't be a surprise, right?'

He nodded again, but his thoughts seemed to have moved on to something else. 'Esmie, does Matty ever complain to you about the amount of babysitting . . . I mean childminding . . . I ask him to do? Looking after you every day after school, I mean?'

'Well . . .' The truth was that Matty was always complaining about having to look after me. But I didn't want Dad to think he'd driven Matthew away by making him do too much babysitting-I-mean-childminding, because I knew that wasn't the case. 'I don't see why he *should* mind,' I answered truthfully. 'I mean, he *has* to stay in after school anyway to do his homework. And it's not like he has to look after me much at the weekends or any other times, is it?'

'Hmm . . . It's just, I sometimes feel like I'm always having a go at him for what he does wrong,' Dad murmured. 'And that maybe I don't praise him enough for the things he does right.'

'Matty knows you really love him, Dad,' I told him.

Dad didn't say anything.

'You know when Juliette was here?' I continued doggedly. 'She used to tell Matty whenever he was moaning about you . . . not that he moaned about you *all* the time or anything . . . that you only grounded him and told him off about stuff because you cared about him so much.' I felt a sudden pang of longing for Juliette, who had always had the answer – or at least *an* answer – to everything. I could hear her now, saying to my brother in her soothing French accent, 'Your father gets anxious about you, Matthew. When you are late home he thinks you are murdered, no? So of course he will *freak out*, as you say . . . You cannot expect him to stay calm while he thinks you are dead in a *deetch*!' Being dead in a ditch was an expression Dad used a lot when he was imagining where my overdue brother might be, and Juliette had quickly adopted it as a favourite of hers.

Dad raised an eyebrow. 'Mary Poppins, eat your heart out,' he grunted. Dad used to call Juliette that when she was here. Juliette *had* been a bit like Mary Poppins in a way, I suppose. She'd been bossy and fun at the same time, and kind of magical in that she seemed to be able to make things happen that nobody else could – like putting an advert in the Lonely Hearts column to find Dad a girlfriend so that he could be less lonely and Matthew and I could have a new mum. Maybe now that she was gone, the magic had gone too – and that was why everything was falling apart.

'You know what, Dad?' I said, desperate to cheer

him up. 'I'll *never* run away from home like Matthew's done!'

'I'm very pleased to hear it,' Dad said, giving me a hug.

'Not even if I fall in love with a boy who's much older than me that I really fancy, who really wants me to run away to Scotland with him to get married and—'

'Esmie,' Dad interrupted, wincing slightly. 'Let's just not go there, OK?'

The following day, after school, I caught the bus straight into town. Holly had brought two disguises to school with her and told me that one was for me and one was for herself. She reckoned she ought to come with me to help tail Lizzie because she said that proper detectives always worked in pairs.

Well, there was no way *that* was going to happen. I told her I wanted to follow Lizzie on my own as I thought that one person wearing a long blonde wig and thick spectacles would look less suspicious than two. Then I noticed that the spectacles she'd brought for herself to wear were actually quite trendy sunglasses, so I quickly took them for myself and gave her back her granny's ultra-hideous ones.

I tried on the least-tangled wig in the girls' toilets. It looked really daft until Holly produced a black woolly hat from her bag and suggested I wore that too. Then the whole thing worked better – though I still looked like what my granny in Bournemouth would call 'a mighty suspicious character'.

'You'll have to keep a safe distance behind Lizzie the whole time, so she doesn't spot you,' Holly warned me, as if *she* was the one who'd been studying how to be a detective, not me. 'And have you planned how you're going to get on the same bus as her without being seen?'

'That's easy – I'll just stand behind somebody tall!' I said dismissively. In fact, I didn't reckon it was going to be easy at all, but I wanted to stop Holly acting like this was *her* undercover operation rather than mine.

I didn't put on my disguise straight away, of course. I had to go and visit Lizzie at work first. As I sat on the bus on my way into town, I thought about the very first time I'd been to see Lizzie at the chemist's last year. Matthew and I had gone there together when we'd been trying to get her to go on a date with Dad. It seemed such a waste now – all the effort we'd put into matchmaking the two of them. Matthew and Juliette and I had all thought Lizzie would be perfect for Dad – but we'd been wrong. If only Juliette was here now, I thought. At least then I wouldn't feel like I was having to do this all on my own.

Lizzie looked surprised when I walked into the shop. She was at the back in the little pharmacy bit, but she came out front as soon as she saw me. 'Hello, Esmie. Is everything all right? Have you heard any more from Matthew?'

I shook my head, but I must have not looked very convincing or something because she added, 'Esmie, you would tell us if he phoned you, wouldn't you? Even if he asked you not to. It's really important that we know he's OK.'

'Dad knows that anyway,' I pointed out. 'Matty told him he was OK in that message he left.'

'I know but—' A customer came and handed in a prescription at that point, so Lizzie had to go back into the pharmacy to sort it out.

By twenty to five I'd been fed lemonade and biscuits twice, and the girl on the till – who looked about Matty's age – was beginning to look as bored as Matty does when I've been chattering away to *him* for ages. Lizzie was starting to look edgy as she eyed her watch.

'I've got to be somewhere else at five o'clock, Esmie,' she said eventually. 'How are you getting back home?'

'I'll catch the bus,' I said. 'Where are you going?'

'Just to an appointment.'

'With who?' I asked her, all innocent-like.

'Oh . . . it's just a . . . a sort of doctor's appointment,' she mumbled.

'*Really?*' I knew that was a complete lie and that made me feel crosser – and braver. 'So what's wrong with you then?' I snapped.

'Don't speak to me like that, Esmie!' Lizzie said, frowning.

I flushed then, because Lizzie had never told me off like that before, sort of like she was my parent. It made me feel even more like she could be my mother. And I realized then that, despite everything, that was still what I really wanted her to be.

'It's nothing to worry about,' Lizzie added more calmly. 'I'm not ill or anything.'

I didn't reply. I couldn't. I felt like I might be going to cry.

We walked to the bus station together in silence.

'Esmie, is something wrong?' Lizzie asked me when we were almost there, but I just shook my head and told her I was off to catch the bus home now and I'd see her later.

After we parted, I watched to see where she went. When I saw her join a queue of people waiting at an empty bus stand across the other side of the station, I quickly slipped off to the toilets to put on my wig, my dark glasses and my woolly hat.

I had a mackintosh rolled up in my bag – also courtesy of Holly's gran – and I slipped that on over my school clothes. By the time I got back, Lizzie's bus had pulled in and the last people in the queue were boarding it. I couldn't see Lizzie so I guessed she must have already got on.

'What's this? Fancy dress?' the bus driver grunted at me as I handed him my fare.

I kept my head down and didn't reply.

I was lucky. Lizzie was sitting quite near the front of the bus but she wasn't looking at any of the other passengers. She seemed to be lost in thought as she stared out of the window. I walked right past her and was able to sit a short way behind her, in an aisle seat, which meant I could easily jump up and follow her when she got off.

The bus took us across town and on to the ring road, past the cemetery where my mother's grave is. Ten minutes later, as we turned off into a more residential area, Lizzie stood up to get off. Several other people got off at that stop too, which was also lucky because it meant it was easy for me to hide behind them.

I waited at the bus stop after the bus drove away, pretending to tie up my shoelace. Lizzie had set off up the road and I wanted to give her a head start. I remembered how my detective book said you should always count to thirty before you started following your suspect.

It wasn't long before Lizzie turned into another street and I had to hurry so as not to lose her. When I turned into that street myself, I saw her disappearing into someone's driveway a short distance along. By the time I got there, Lizzie had walked up to the front door of the house and was waiting inside the porch. The house was a big, old-looking one with large windows and, as I hid behind the hedge to watch, I saw the front door being opened by a slim, tall man about the same age as my dad. He had short, dark hair and he smiled at Lizzie as he let her inside. The door closed behind them quickly, but a minute or two later I saw Lizzie again through the window, in the room to the left of the front door. I decided to sneak up closer to the house to see better.

I positioned myself in a flower bed, standing just to one side of the window, worrying fleetingly that I was leaving suspicious footprints like the ones my detective book says criminals are always leaving in flower beds. But since I wasn't a criminal, I decided it probably didn't matter.

The room Lizzie was in had a leather sofa and a big leather armchair, and there was a desk in the corner with a pile of papers on it. Andrew hadn't come into the room yet. Lizzie was sitting down with her back resting against one arm of the sofa, looking like she was about to put her feet up, just like you'd do if you knew the person you were visiting really well. And then she did the thing that made me totally unable to hold it together any longer.

She kicked off her shoes!

My vision seemed to go blurry and my heart started racing and suddenly I had this horrible image inside my head of Andrew coming into the room, sitting down next to her on the sofa, kicking off his own shoes, putting his arms round her and *kissing* her.

I wanted to shout out in protest, but I couldn't seem to find my voice and before I knew what I was doing I was banging really hard on the window.

Lizzie nearly jumped out of her skin. She leapt up, tripping over her shoes as she called out loudly, 'Andrew! There's somebody outside!'

I suppose I shouldn't have been surprised that she didn't recognize me.

By the time Andrew opened the front door – with Lizzie standing right behind him in the hall – I had pulled off the wig and the woolly hat and taken off the sunglasses.

'Esmie!' Lizzie gasped. She pushed past Andrew, stepping out of the front door towards me, but she couldn't get very far on the gravel drive because she wasn't wearing her shoes.

I pointed to her feet. My hand was trembling. 'Does Dad *know* you . . . you . . . go around taking off your shoes in other men's houses?' I spluttered.

And before she had time to reply, I had turned and fled.

By the time I got home I was all fired up and ready to tell Dad everything.

Dad was in the kitchen making himself a mug of coffee and I went to join him immediately. But before I could open my mouth, the doorbell rang and there was the sound of a key in the lock. I knew it was Lizzie because she's the only one who rings our bell *as well* as letting herself in with the key Dad has had cut for her. I looked out of the window and saw a taxi pulling away and guessed that she must have called one from Andrew's to try and get back before I did.

'Lizzie's having an affair, Dad,' I blurted out before she could get through the door.

Dad nearly choked on a mouthful of coffee. By the time he'd finished coughing, Lizzie had come into the kitchen.

I turned on her immediately. 'I saw you in that

man's house!' I yelled. 'I saw you taking off your shoes!'

'Esmie, listen . . .' Lizzie started to say, but I wouldn't let her talk.

'You lied about where you were going! You said you were going to the doctor's when you were going to *his* house!'

'Esmie, what are you talking about?' Dad was staring at me as if he thought I'd gone mad. I suppose I shouldn't have expected him to take me seriously straight away. After all, he hadn't seen what *I'd* seen, had he?

I was about to describe *exactly* what I'd seen, when we heard a noise in the hall.

We turned around.

'Matty!' I gasped. Matthew was standing in the kitchen doorway and the first thing I thought was that I'd forgotten he had a broken arm. He looked a bit scruffier than usual, but apart from that he was just the same. I reminded myself that he'd only been gone a few days – it just *felt* like longer.

'Hi,' he grunted.

I ran over and hugged him – even though he didn't deserve it. I couldn't help it.

When I stepped back, I saw that my brother was looking warily at Dad, who had seemed to freeze when Matty appeared.

'I'm sorry, Dad,' Matthew said nervously.

Dad was nodding slowly. 'So you should be.'

Then Dad stepped forward and the next minute he had his arms round my brother and was holding him really tightly.

My head felt a bit swimmy. I was pleased that my brother was home again, but I still felt terrible about Lizzie.

It seemed to take Dad and Matthew several minutes before they felt ready to let go of each other, but when they did, Dad immediately switched into stern parent mode. '*Where the hell have you been?*'

But Lizzie spoke before Matthew could answer. 'Esmie and I need to talk, John, and so do you and Matthew. Why don't you go through to the living room, and Esmie and I can stay in here?'

Dad glanced at us as if he was just starting to recollect – but only vaguely – what had been taking place before my brother's arrival. 'Fine,' he muttered. He put one hand on my brother's shoulder. 'Come on.'

'Jennifer's waiting outside,' my brother mumbled.

'Well, we'd better invite her in so that she can phone *her* father and put *him* out of his misery too, hadn't we?' Dad said.

So Matty went off with Dad to fetch Jennifer, and I stayed in the kitchen with Lizzie.

Lizzie sat down at one side of the table and pointed to the seat opposite her. I stayed standing. If she thought she could talk her way out of this, she was wrong.

Lizzie sighed. 'Esmie, the man you saw me with today . . . Andrew . . . it's not what you think . . . You see . . . he's my psychotherapist.' She paused. 'Do you know what that is?'

I gaped at her. For a moment I thought she was lying to me. Then I knew that she couldn't be, because no one would ever make up something as crazy as that. '*Psychotherapist?*'

'That's right.'

'You mean he's not your . . . ?' I trailed off, finding it hard to take this in.

'Of course not! I've been seeing Andrew for an hour every week for a couple of months now. I didn't tell you I had an appointment with him today because . . . well . . . I felt like it was something I wanted to keep private.' She looked at me. 'Somehow you seem to have got completely the wrong idea.'

'I thought . . .' I suddenly found my voice drying up and my eyes filling with tears.

Lizzie got up and came to put her arm round me. 'I'm sorry I scared you, Esmie. I had no idea.'

'B-but you took off your shoes in his house,' I stammered dumbly.

'In order to lie down on his couch! It's a therapy couch, Esmie. Actually, I think it's a bit unnecessary myself, but since that's the way he likes to do it . . .'

I sniffed. I knew all about therapy couches. I had seen a film once where this weirdo therapist got his patients to lie on his couch and then he hypnotized them into going off and murdering all the people he didn't like.

I sniffed some more and Lizzie got me to sit down while she fetched me a glass of water. Other thoughts were starting to stir in my mind. Lizzie wasn't having an affair, but she *was* seeing a psychotherapist.

'Does he hypnotize you?' I blurted out as she handed me the water.

'Pardon?'

'Andrew . . . does he *hypnotize* you?'

Lizzie looked slightly amused. 'No – he just listens to me talking. It's a bit like going to see a counsellor.'

'Like Holly's mum?'

'Like Holly's mum . . . only he digs a bit deeper . . . goes more into your past . . . what happened when you were younger and stuff . . . to try and help you understand why you're feeling the way you are now. It's kind of complicated, Esmie. It probably doesn't make much sense to you, does it?'

I shook my head. What made the least sense was what worries Lizzie could have that were so bad that she had to go and be therapized – though thankfully not *hypnotized* – about them.

'Lizzie, you're not *dying* or anything, are you?' Goodness knows why I said that. It was the worst possible worry I could think of anyone having, I suppose.

'No, of course not! And I'm not *ill* either. Like I said, Andrew is a type of doctor – but he's the type who helps you with problems that are . . . well, that are stopping you from getting on with your life. Andrew helped me a few years ago when I got depressed after my father died. So when I started not knowing what to do about . . .' She swallowed. 'Well, when there was something else I needed help with in my life, I decided to go back to him.'

'Why didn't you tell Dad you were going to see him?' I asked.

'Why do you think?'

I thought about Dad's views on therapy and thought that, if I were Lizzie, I probably wouldn't have wanted to tell him either.

Lizzie gave a wry smile as she added, 'I was sure

John would freak out if he thought I was talking about him . . . I mean, talking about *things* . . . to a complete stranger. But I'll tell him now and he's just going to have to accept it, isn't he?'

I nodded. But it still didn't seem right somehow, her having to go behind Dad's back like that in the first place instead of being able to talk to him. 'Lizzie, what is it that you don't know what to do about?'

She shook her head. 'Enough questions, Esmie.'

'Are you worried Dad doesn't give you enough juicy compliments and stuff?' It was the only thing I could think of. 'Cos that's not because he doesn't like you – it's because he's from Mars. I read all about it in this book called *Men Are from Mars, Women Are from Venus*. It's meant to be for grown-ups, but Holly and I sneaked a look at it. It tells you how men and women act like they're from different planets.'

Lizzie gave a short laugh, though I didn't really see what there was to laugh about. 'Listen, Esmie . . . my problems aren't something for you to worry about. So just you leave this for me and your dad to sort out, OK?'

'So it *is* to do with Dad then?' I said swiftly.

Before she could answer, we heard Dad's voice raised in the other room. I wondered, fleetingly, what was happening to Matthew and Jennifer. Not that I felt too worried about my brother. As far as I was concerned, whatever punishment he got, he fully deserved. If he was grounded for a year then I reckoned it'd serve him right.

Just as I was thinking that, Dad opened the living-room door. 'Esmie, we need you in here for a minute, please.'

Lizzie quickly said she had to go to the bathroom and dodged out of the kitchen, no doubt to escape any further interrogation from me.

I followed Dad into the living room.

I had almost forgotten that the skeleton-in-the-allotments saga was what had made Jennifer run away with Matthew in the first place, so when Dad said, 'Esmie, I think you've got something to say to Jennifer, haven't you?' I didn't immediately know what he meant, plus my mind was still on my conversation with Lizzie.

'It's OK,' Jennifer said quickly. 'After all, it was *possible* that it could have been my mum. She doesn't have to apologize.'

'I think she *does*,' Dad said, looking at me sternly.

That's when I twigged what they were on about. 'Sorry,' I said quickly, thinking that I'd already apologized once about that skeleton mix-up over the phone. But maybe Jennifer hadn't told Dad about that phone call – or about the real reason they'd come back.

'If you'd stayed and asked *me* about it, Jennifer, I could have *told* you the whole thing was nonsense,' Dad said.

'I know. I'm sorry,' Jennifer mumbled, avoiding looking at him. 'Matty told me Esmie gets really silly ideas into her head sometimes . . .' She trailed off as she noticed me glaring at her.

I shifted my glare to my brother.

'Well, you do, Ez!' Matthew said defensively. 'What about when we went to see *The Sound of Music* and you thought that Dad and Juliette were going to fall in love and get married, just because it happened to the father and the nanny in the film? You're always making huge dramas out of stuff. Every time you get a headache you reckon you've got meningitis and you start telling us who you want to be invited to your funeral—'

'That's not true!' I snarled. (Though I *do* have a funeral 'A' list *and* a list of reserves.)

'OK, that's enough!' Dad snapped at both of us. 'If this is a competition for drama queens, Matthew, then running away from home has got to be the winner.' The doorbell rang and Matty jumped up to answer it (and escape from Dad, I reckon), but Dad wasn't in a mood to be escaped from. He told my brother to keep his backside parked right where it was if he knew what was good for him – and it.

The second Dad left the room to go to the door, Jennifer started bombarding me with questions and I felt like telling her to shut-up. I certainly didn't feel like telling her anything about her aunt or like handing over that phone number – not until I got a bit of respect from the two of them. I was about to tell them that when a gruff voice made us all jump.

'*Jennifer!*' Mr Mitchell was standing in the doorway.

'*Dad!*' Jennifer just stared at him.

Neither of them seemed to know what to say to each other after that. Mr Mitchell certainly didn't try to hug Jennifer like Dad had hugged Matty, which was probably just as well because Jennifer looked like she was ready to back away from him if he came any closer.

Dad quickly invited Mr Mitchell to sit down and join us and I half-expected to be ejected from the room at that point, but for some reason – maybe Dad forgot – I wasn't. Lizzie was still keeping completely out of the way, I noticed.

Thankfully, nobody mentioned anything about the skeleton-in-the-allotments. Maybe Jennifer was going to tell her dad what I'd accused him of later or maybe she wasn't, but for the moment she just launched into accusing him of stuff herself. She told him that the reason she'd run away from home was because he'd forbidden her to try and find her mother and forbidden her to see my brother, and that she'd got fed up with being forbidden to do everything. 'I'm not your *property*, Dad!' she spat out angrily. 'This isn't the Middle Ages!'

'I was only thinking of what was best for you—'

'No you weren't! You were thinking what was best for *you*! Anyway, I'm not coming home! I told you that on the phone!'

'Of course you're coming home! Where else are you going to go?'

And that's when Jennifer looked at Matthew – and my heart missed a beat.

So did Matthew's, judging by the look on his face, even though this was something they'd clearly discussed before coming back. 'Dad . . .' he began, turning to look at our father, whose face had become very wary all of a sudden. 'Jen doesn't want to go home so I said . . . I said she could stay here with us.' He swallowed hard and waited, like he really wanted Dad to say something. When Dad didn't, he continued in a rush, 'But if that's not cool with you, it's OK. I'll give up school and find a job, and so will she, and we'll rent somewhere to live together.'

'Don't be ridiculous!' Mr Mitchell snapped.

Dad was staring at my brother. 'Give up school?'

'Dad, try and understand . . .' Matthew's voice had gone shaky. 'It's just . . .' He didn't seem able to finish.

'Just *what*?' Dad glared at him. 'An *ultimatum*?'

Matthew looked terrible, like he wanted to disappear. Pink blotches were starting to appear on his cheeks.

Jennifer jumped up and pulled my brother with her. 'Come on, Matthew. We don't have to stay here.'

'Jennifer, sit down!' Mr Mitchell barked.

'I'm not a dog, Dad!' Jennifer snapped back as she started towards the door. Matthew followed her, glancing at Dad, who suddenly seemed to spring into action.

'OK,' Dad said. 'You can both stay here.'

Matthew paused but Jennifer didn't.

'Wait, Jen,' my brother said.

'I don't want to stay where I'm not wanted, Matthew,' Jennifer told him, and it was obvious that she was fighting back tears as she continued to head for the front door.

Dad stood up then. 'But I *want* you to stay, Jennifer! Matthew's right. I'd much rather have you both here than out on the streets.'

But Jennifer was shaking her head. 'Matthew,

you stay here if you want,' she gasped, starting to open our front door. 'It's OK. Really.' Tears were starting to run down her face.

'Of course I'm not staying if you're not!' Matthew burst out, following her. And I thought how this really was just like a scene from *Romeo and Juliet.*

'Wait a minute, Matthew,' Dad called out after him. 'Do you have any money?'

Mr Mitchell practically exploded. 'You want to give them *money* to run away with?'

Dad ignored him. He kept looking at Matthew, who had stopped now and was shaking his head. Dad looked like he was thinking very rapidly. 'I think the best place for you to stay until we sort this out is the youth hostel in town. I can phone them now and book you a room each on my credit card. OK?'

Matthew nodded, looking surprised. 'OK . . . Thanks, Dad . . .'

'But in return I want you to ring me tomorrow and let me know how you're doing. Is that clear?'

Matthew nodded again.

Jennifer was at the bottom of our drive now and my brother hurried after her.

'Jennifer, don't go!' Mr Mitchell suddenly cried out, sounding like he was starting to panic. 'I need

to tell you something . . . It's about your mother . . .
There's something you don't know . . .'

But Jennifer didn't look back.

I told Holly everything that had happened with Matthew and Jennifer as we sat next to each other in the lunch hall at school the next day.

I also told her the new information about the skeleton in the allotments, which Dad had finally released to me at breakfast this morning. (He was going to release it to the rest of the world later in the day.)

'Dad says the skeleton belongs to a woman who was reported missing ten years ago,' I said. 'She was a bit of a recluse or something and she sort of disappeared from her house and nobody knew where she'd gone. They still don't know how she ended up in the allotments, so they're putting out an appeal for information about her on the news today. Dad's not getting to go on TV though.'

'That's a shame.'

'I know.' I'm always telling Dad that I wish he could be on TV more often, but he says he's quite happy to avoid speaking to reporters whenever possible, thanks very much.

'So is Jennifer still looking for her mum?'

'I don't know. I still haven't given her the phone number for her aunt. I don't know what do if she asks me for it now. I could make her and Matthew come back again to get it, but they might just go away the minute I hand it over.'

'*I* can't believe that your dad just *let* Matthew go off like that!'

'I know, but Dad says this was the only way he could think of to keep some sort of control over the situation. He says at least this way he knows exactly where Matty is. And he's going to tell Matty that he's got to go back to school.'

'This is all Jennifer's fault,' Holly said sharply. 'She's a bad influence!'

I giggled. 'You sound like my granny.'

'Well, she's totally unsuitable for him. Anyone can see that!'

'Holly, he's never going to look at *you*, anyway!' I burst out. 'You're only twelve.'

'I'm not expecting him to look at me *yet*. But I was reading this article about how people who've known each other as kids can fall in love with each other as adults and—'

'Listen, Holly, there's something I need you to ask your mum for me,' I interrupted her quickly.

'Can you ask her *why* people like Lizzie go and see therapists?' Lizzie hadn't stayed the night at ours last night and when I'd seen Dad briefly at breakfast this morning, he'd said that she'd told him about Andrew and she was coming round tonight so that they could talk about it some more. Not that he would then be talking to *me* about it, he'd added swiftly, since this was Lizzie's business – not mine and Holly's. ('I wouldn't tell *Holly* anything!' I'd said indignantly, but he'd just raised an eyebrow like he thought that was most unlikely.)

Holly promised she'd ask her mum for me and that she'd phone me with the answer tonight.

I decided to phone Juliette to ask her the same question when I got home from school.

'Esmie? How are you?' Hearing Juliette's voice was so comforting that I immediately blurted out the whole Matthew story and the whole Lizzie story and found myself adding, 'Everything's gone wrong since you left, Juliette. Can't you come back and be our au pair again? Then everything will be OK!'

'Of course it will not be OK. It will be much worse. You know how your father hates to have me interfering.'

'That never stopped you before!' I protested.

'It was my job before. Like it was Mary Poppins's job, no?' She knew all about how we'd always likened her to Mary Poppins. 'But now it is not my job and I must certainly not give my interfering to your father. It will make him much more angry.'

'Well, can you give your interfering to *me*, please?' I asked desperately. 'Just tell me why *you* think Lizzie might be seeing a psychotherapist.'

Juliette snorted like she thought I was making a big fuss about nothing. 'It is perfectly *normal* to see a therapist. In France we do it all the time.'

'Yes, but *why*, Juliette?'

'Well . . . people see therapists to talk about themselves . . . sometimes they want to talk because their life is not how they want it. Or because they are trying to make a big decision and it is it difficult for them to do it on their own.'

'A big decision?' I immediately thought about how big a decision it was to get married to someone – especially when it meant taking on their two kids as well.

'Have you asked *her* why she is going?'

'Yes, but she wouldn't tell me.' I paused. 'I think it might be something to do with Dad.'

'Hmm . . . Any sign that they will move in together?'

'No.'

'Perhaps Lizzie wants more commitment from your father before she does that. Perhaps she wants to get married first.'

'There's no sign of that either,' I said gloomily.

'And Matthew? You say he is staying at this youth hostel now? It is very basic there compared with home, no? I think he will soon be back.'

'But Jennifer's there too,' I pointed out.

'Ah . . .' Juliette sounded like she had to admit that was a problem.

Matthew didn't say anything about coming home soon when he rang us from his mobile that evening. I heard Dad offer to keep paying for the youth hostel so long as he kept ringing home each day, and then Dad called out to me that Matthew wanted to speak to me.

No prizes for guessing what that was about. 'Tell him if he wants to speak to me he'll have to come and see me,' I'd called back stroppily.

Holly phoned me later, after Lizzie got here, and I spoke to her on the telephone in Dad's bedroom. But Holly couldn't really add much to what Juliette had already told me about why people saw therapists. 'But listen, I just read this magazine article that made me think of you especially,' she added. 'It said how it can be difficult taking on a new partner with lots of baggage – and that step-kids are *mega*-baggage. So maybe that's what Lizzie's worried about.'

'Great,' I said drily. Matthew and I certainly

came along with Dad as part of the package –
there was no doubt about that. But *mega-baggage*?

'Where's Lizzie?' I asked Dad when I went
downstairs a bit later on.

'She's gone home.'

'Already?' I frowned. 'Dad, is Lizzie going to see
a therapist because she's unsure about marrying
you, and is she unsure about marrying you,
because she thinks stepchildren are baggage?'

Dad looked startled. 'Where did this come
from?'

'Is she, Dad?'

'Sweetheart, of course Lizzie doesn't see you as
baggage. Lizzie *wants* to be your mum. She *loves* the
idea of motherhood!'

'Then why hasn't she had any children herself?'
I demanded.

Dad grunted something under his breath, which
I didn't hear properly. But I thought it sounded
like, 'Give her time.'

'Does Lizzie *want* children then?' I persisted,
feeling more hopeful at the thought that she might.
'Cos if you and her got married –' I broke off as I
saw the look on his face.

'You don't want Lizzie to have a baby, do you,
Dad?' I was staring at him.

He was avoiding looking at me. 'Don't you think
it's time you were getting ready for bed?'

'But, Dad, *why* don't you want to have—'

'Just go to bed now, Esmie. It's late.'

My mind was racing. Lizzie wanted a baby and Dad didn't. Was *that* the problem then? Was *that* the reason Lizzie was going to see a therapist?

As I lay in bed I thought about how Holly had told me that her mum saw couples together so they could talk about their problems and how that often stopped them from splitting up. I was still awake and thinking about it half an hour later when Dad put his head round my door because my light was still on.

'Esmie, you should be asleep. You've got school tomorrow.'

I sat up in bed. I knew it was a long shot, but it was worth a try . . . 'Dad, why don't you go and see Lizzie's therapist with her so the two of you can talk about having babies *together*?' I suggested. 'Or not having them,' I added quickly, because Dad was really glaring at me now.

'Esmie, I would rather *give birth* to a baby than lie on a couch like some neurotic character out of a Woody Allen film and be therapized by some wacko shrink. Now turn out that light!'

'Andrew isn't a wacko,' I protested. Since I don't watch Woody Allen films, I wasn't sure what he meant by that, but I added firmly, 'And it doesn't mean you're *neurotic* if you go and see him.

Juliette says people in France go and see therapists all the time and that everybody in France is normal.'

'*Juliette* says?'

'Not that I've discussed it with her or anything,' I added. And I quickly turned out my light and pulled my duvet up over my head to show that I was more than ready to go to sleep now.

Juliette phoned me the next evening to see how I was. Dad picked up the phone first and I was scared the two of them would start talking – and arguing – but they didn't. Dad just handed the phone straight over to me and left the room, looking like he felt a bit embarrassed.

'How are things?' Juliette asked me.

'Not good,' I replied gloomily. 'Dad doesn't want another baby and Lizzie does, so I think that's the reason they're not getting on and Lizzie is going to see a therapist.'

'Really?' Juliette sounded interested. 'Well . . . I can see that for Lizzie this is a problem . . . She is how old? Thirty-eight? Thirty-nine? The time is running out for her to have a baby, no?'

'I suppose.' I'd never actually thought before about what Lizzie's age meant in terms of her being able to have babies.

'I wonder why your father is so against it . . .

Perhaps he is worried that *you* would not cope very well with another baby in the family . . .'

'You think it's because of *me* that he doesn't want one?'

'I am just saying it may be because of what he *thinks* it will mean for you. In fact, it would be good for you *not* to be the baby of the family and have all the attention all the time, no?'

'I do *not* have all the attention all the time!' I retorted hotly.

'Hmm . . .' Juliette sounded like she didn't agree. 'Anyway, this is not about what *you* want. It is about what your father wants. So there is nothing you can do about it.'

'But if *he* wants what he thinks *I* want, then it *is* about what I want, isn't it?' I protested. 'So there *is* something I can do about it!'

'Say again.' Juliette sounded confused – not surprisingly when you think that English is only her second language.

'What if I *tell* Dad I really *want* a baby brother or sister?' I said. A plan was already beginning to form in my mind and I quickly said goodbye to Juliette and punched in Holly's phone number instead.

'Holly, you know how I never got to come round to yours to see your cousin because of Matthew running away and everything? Well, do you think you could get your mum to bring her round here this weekend instead?' I asked her breathlessly. Holly was always going on about how all her mum's friends – the men as well as the women – got really broody the second they clapped eyes on her baby cousin. So I reckoned if seeing *her* didn't change Dad's mind about having another baby, then nothing would.

The following evening Matthew and Jennifer arrived unannounced on our front doorstep. Matthew said he wanted to collect some things and, since Dad followed him upstairs so he could talk to him, I got left on my own with Jennifer.

'Esmie, please can you give me my aunt's phone number?' she asked me as soon as Dad was out of earshot.

'It's upstairs.'

'Well, can you go and get it?' She smiled at me and I was reminded of how much I'd liked her before she'd got Matthew to leave home with her. 'Please?'

I didn't see any way out of giving her what she wanted now.

I was in my bedroom and had just picked up the piece of paper with the number on it, when Dad suddenly appeared in my doorway. I didn't see him at first because I was busy studying the number and trying to memorize it. I reckoned that was a precaution any decent detective would take before they handed over such an important piece of information.

'What are you doing, Esmie?'

'Nothing!' But I must have looked guilty because he came right over to me.

'What's that?' He was looking at the paper in my hand.

'Just a phone number,' I mumbled.

'Whose phone number?'

Matthew was standing behind Dad now, carrying the little rucksack he uses when he goes away for weekends. 'Jennifer's aunt's,' he blurted out impatiently, as if he was fed up with trying to keep it a secret any more. 'And Jennifer's got a right to have it, which means Esmie can stop mucking around and just hand it over.'

'It's not up to you, Matthew!' I retaliated sharply. 'This phone number belongs to me. I'm the one who found it, remember? So it's my decision whether I give it to Jennifer or not!'

My brother made a lunge for the piece of paper, which I briefly thought of swallowing like they do in spy movies when they want to stop secret evidence getting into the wrong hands. But I was scared that if I did I might a) forget the number and b) choke to death. So I shoved the piece of paper into the back pocket of my jeans instead.

Dad was looking mystified as he watched the two of us. 'I don't understand. What's the big deal about this phone number?'

But Jennifer had come up the stairs now to find out what was going on, and Dad quickly launched into telling her that her father really wanted to talk to her and that he thought she should let him.

Jennifer shook her head dismissively. 'I don't want to see him. Esmie, have you got that number?'

'Yes, but . . .' I broke off. Dad was signalling to me that he didn't want me to give it to her just yet. I didn't know what to do. After all, Dad is a Detective Chief Inspector and I'm only . . . Well, let's face it, I'm not even a proper *low*-ranking detective yet!

'Esmie . . . *please* . . .' Jennifer was looking straight at me and her eyes were pleading. She lowered her voice to a whisper. 'You said you wanted to help me because you know what it's like not to have a mum . . .'

I felt terrible then. A real traitor. But I suddenly thought of another reason why Jennifer needed to do what Dad said. 'Your Aunt Helen said she wouldn't speak to you unless your dad knew you were phoning her. So I think you'll have to talk to him anyway, Jennifer.'

'Why not let me phone him now and ask him to come round?' Dad suggested quickly. 'Then you can tell him about your aunt, and he can tell you whatever it is that he needs to tell you. Then Esmie can give you that phone number and you and Matthew can either go back to the hostel or – and I mean this – you can both move in here until we think of a better alternative. You're more than welcome to have Juliette's old room, Jennifer.'

'That'd be great, Dad,' Matthew blurted out. He looked at Jennifer hopefully – and Jennifer couldn't miss seeing how badly *he* wanted to come home again at any rate.

'Oh, Matthew,' she sighed, looking at my brother in a way that made me think that at long last she might be feeling a bit guilty about tearing him away from us. She looked at our father. 'I'll hear Dad out, if that's what the deal is, but I'm not going back home with him no matter how hard he tries to make me, OK?'

'I told you, Jennifer,' Dad replied calmly, 'after you've listened to him – if you still want to – you can move in here with us.'

*

'Jennifer, I think you and I need to talk on our own,' Mr Mitchell said as soon as Dad had brought him into the living room to join the rest of us.

'No way!' She looked at him distrustfully, leaning closer to my brother, who was sitting beside her on the sofa.

He sighed. 'All right then . . . If this is the way you want it . . .' He paused. 'Jennifer, there's something I need to tell you about your mother. It's about that letter—'

'The one *you* wrote, you mean?' Jennifer snapped. 'You already told me about that. You told me you wrote it because you wanted me to grow up *thinking* she cared about me, when really she . . .' Jennifer's voice gave out and my brother put his arm round her.

'Jennifer, listen to me . . .' Mr Mitchell was sounding shaky himself now. He came over and crouched down beside her. 'The thing is . . . your mother *did* write you a letter after she left.'

'No she didn't.' Jennifer's eyes were filling up. '*You* wrote it. It's your handwriting. You've already admitted that.'

'She *did* write to you and the thing is . . . the thing is . . . I was so angry with her, I tore it up. Later I regretted it and that's when I wrote that other letter for you . . . as a replacement.'

Jennifer gaped at him.

185

'I lied to you about it the other day because I wanted to discourage you from looking for her. I didn't know how she'd react if you found her. And I didn't want you to get hurt.' He paused. 'But I realize now that I can't stop you looking for her if it's what you really want. So I'd rather *help* you than . . .' He trailed off.

'*Lose you*,' Dad finished for him, glancing sideways at Matthew.

Jennifer was staring speechlessly at her father. 'What did it say?' she finally whispered hoarsely. 'Her real letter?'

Mr Mitchell frowned. 'That she wanted to take you with her but she didn't think she'd be able to look after you properly. That she felt like she wouldn't be any good to you as a mother. Things like that.' There was a brief silence, then he added, 'I haven't a clue where she is now though, Jennifer. I'm as much in the dark about that as you are.'

And that's when Jennifer mumbled, 'But Esmie isn't.'

'*Esmie?*' Mr Mitchell looked at me in surprise.

When Jennifer didn't seem able to say anything else, Matthew spoke. 'Esmie's managed to track down Jennifer's aunt, so we're hoping *she* might be able to help us.'

'I don't understand.' Mr Mitchell was staring at

me as if Matthew had just announced I could fly or something.

'Neither do I,' Dad said. 'Esmie, how did *you* manage to find Jennifer's aunt?'

So I told them how I'd managed to find the right Doctor Helen Forbes – and a wrong one – by looking up her name in the medical register in the library.

'How on earth did you know to do that?' Dad asked.

I remembered how Lizzie had given me the lead about the medical register. 'It sort of came up during the course of another investigation,' I explained.

'Another *investigation*?'

'Yes. You see, I want to be a detective like you when I grow up, Dad,' I told him, to clarify things. 'So I've been practising.'

The following Sunday, Jennifer came round to tell us that she'd spoken to her aunt on the phone the previous day and that they were going to meet next week. Things were still difficult between Jennifer and her dad but, now that he'd agreed that she could search for her mother if she wanted, she had decided to move back home again. Jennifer's dad wasn't trying to stop her seeing Matthew any more either (much to Holly's disappointment).

'I keep telling Dad that I'm not going to leave *him*, just because I find *her*,' Jennifer said as she sat with me and Matthew at our kitchen table, drinking Coke and eating our way through a packet of chocolate digestives. 'I really think *that's* what he's most afraid of – not about me getting hurt at all.'

'He did have a point the other day though, didn't he?' Matthew said, frowning. 'About how she could have contacted you at any time if she'd wanted to see you again, because *she* knows where *you* are.'

Jennifer looked uncomfortable. 'Maybe she thinks I wouldn't want to see her if she just turned up like that.'

'Maybe.' Matthew didn't sound convinced and it struck me that he was beginning to sound more like he was on Jennifer's father's side than on Jennifer's.

'Does your aunt have *any* idea where your mum might be?' I asked Jennifer, because I for one still really wanted her to find her mother.

'Not really – she hasn't heard from her in years. But she's got contact details for some old friends of my mum's who might be able to help.'

'Did she tell you much about her?'

Jennifer nodded. 'It sounds like my mum and my aunt had a really tough time being abandoned by *their* mum and dad when they were little. Helen says she thinks my mum never got over it. She says she reckons that could be why she freaked out and couldn't cope with being a parent herself.'

'You'd think the last thing she'd do is abandon her own child after it happened to her,' Matthew grunted.

'Yes, but it isn't that simple,' Jennifer said, frowning.

'How simple is keeping in touch with your own daughter?'

'Well, she tried, but my dad ripped up her letter, didn't he?'

'She could've written some *more* letters. Or come back to see you. I mean, parents split up all the time, but that doesn't mean they don't see their kids any more, does it?'

'I saw a TV programme round at Holly's a while back,' I put in quickly. 'They were interviewing all these kids whose parents had split up and loads of *them* never saw their dads any more.'

'Exactly!' Jennifer said sharply. 'You're just saying it's weird because it was my *mum* who left and not my dad. You're just being sexist, Matthew.'

'No I'm not. I just think that if your own *mother* couldn't be bothered to—'

'Shut up, Matthew!' Jennifer burst out, looking like she was about to start crying.

My brother immediately backed down. 'Jen, I'm sorry. I didn't mean—' But she had already stormed out.

Dad came downstairs then and wanted to know what was going on. Matty was standing in the hall with the front door still open, looking really worried, and I could see he wanted to talk to Dad about what had happened, so I left them to it.

I had other things to think about anyway. Lizzie was coming round for Sunday lunch and I'd arranged for Holly to come round with her mum and her aunt and her aunt's baby – who's called Ella – just afterwards. Holly had assured me that even people who didn't normally like babies could never resist Ella. And this would also give me a chance to show Dad how much I'd just *love* to have a baby in our household myself.

Lizzie arrived and we all had lunch together and, when Dad mentioned that maybe we could go for a walk in the afternoon as it was a really nice day, I quickly told him about our expected visitors. He didn't look at all pleased. Holly and her mum arrived just as we were clearing up the lunch dishes and the second they walked in the door, Matty grunted that he had to go upstairs and finish off his homework. Holly looked really disappointed.

Holly's aunt hadn't come, having decided to take up the offer of free babysitting that afternoon while she escaped to the shops. 'Poor thing, she's totally desperate for some time to herself,' Holly's mum said as soon as they'd got seated.

We all sat gazing at baby Ella who *was* really cute. I sneaked a look at Dad to check out his reaction to her as I crossed the room to give Holly's mum the baby clothes Lizzie and I had bought as a present the other day.

Then Ella started to cry.

And she went on crying.

'Can you take her for a minute while I go and get her stuff out of the car?' Holly's mother said to

Lizzie. She sounded harassed. 'I'd forgotten how much stuff babies need with them wherever they go. It's like packing for a fortnight's holiday every time you step out the front door.'

In a perfect world, Ella would have stopped crying the second Lizzie took her in her arms, showing what a wonderful mother Lizzie was going to be. But Lizzie seemed to make the baby worse by jiggling her about.

'Here,' she said to Dad after she'd had Ella screaming in her ear for several minutes. 'You take her.'

And the second Dad had Ella in *his* arms, she stopped crying.

'Look, Dad!' I said enthusiastically. 'She must really like you!'

Then Ella puked up all over him.

After Dad had got cleaned up, Ella had been changed, and we'd all gulped down cups of tea as fast as we could, Holly's mum said they'd better be getting home so that Ella could have her afternoon nap, because if she missed it she would be a total nightmare to look after for the rest of the day.

The minute they'd left, Dad asked if I'd mind going upstairs for a bit so that Lizzie and he could have some time on their own. I was scared they were going to have a row after I left them together but, strangely enough, the opposite happened. I had just reached the top landing when I heard them burst out laughing.

I lay on my bed, not sure what to think. I couldn't help glancing across at my mother's photo and wondering what she would make of all this. I suddenly thought about how, if she had lived, *she* might have had another baby after me. I'd never asked Dad whether or not they'd been planning to have any more or whether they'd made up their minds to stop at two. And then something else hit me. I couldn't imagine why I hadn't thought of it before.

My mum had *died* giving birth to me, hadn't she? That was how Dad had lost her. So what if the reason he didn't want Lizzie to have a baby was because he was scared he might lose *her* that way too?

It was suddenly all so clear to me that I couldn't wait to make things clear to Lizzie and Dad too. I raced downstairs and burst into the room – catching Dad in the middle of kissing Lizzie on the sofa.

They sprung apart as soon as I came in.

'Listen, Dad,' I blurted out. 'Holly showed me this magazine article ages ago that said how it's easier to get run over by a bus than to die in childbirth these days.'

'Esmie, what are you talking about?' Dad looked confused.

'Or a car,' I added because, now I came to think about it, I wasn't sure the article had said it was common for people to get run over specifically by *buses*.

Dad didn't look any more enlightened.

'I'm talking about how Lizzie *isn't* going to die like my mum did, if she has a baby.' I turned to Lizzie and announced dramatically, 'That's the reason he doesn't want you to have one, Lizzie!'

Dad was sitting up straight now, shaking his head at me and looking perplexed. 'Esmie, stop this!'

'But, Dad, it's obvious that—'

'Esmie, *listen*!' Dad was frowning. 'Of course I'd be more nervous in the delivery room than your average expectant father, but that's not the reason I feel the way I do about having another baby.' He sighed. 'If you must know, it's all the interrupted nights and the endless feeds and the dirty nappies and all that *work* all over again. *That's* what I'm afraid of.'

I was gobsmacked. I looked at Lizzie but she was avoiding my gaze. She didn't look surprised though, so I guessed Dad had already had this conversation with her.

'Didn't you *like* me and Matthew when we were babies then?' I asked in a small voice.

'Of course I did. Just because it was your mother who felt *ready* to have kids, that doesn't mean I wasn't delighted when you both came along. But, quite frankly, the thought of going through all that baby stuff again . . .' He pulled a face.

Lizzie was staring at him. 'So you mean you had to have your arm twisted the first time round as well?'

Dad looked at her warily. 'Yes, but—'

Before he could continue, the phone rang and he swiftly went to answer it.

'Hold on a minute, Jennifer. I'll go and get him,' we heard him say. Matthew had tried to phone Jennifer earlier and she had refused to speak to him. Then he'd wanted to go round there, but Dad had warned him that Jennifer probably needed some time on her own. Now it sounded like Jennifer had decided she was ready to talk to him after all. I only hoped she wasn't phoning to dump him.

'That row with Jennifer wasn't really Matty's fault,' I told Dad when he came back into the living room. 'He was only thinking about *her*. I mean, it must be horrible knowing your mum left you when you were little. That's why Matty said those things about her – because he doesn't think she should have done that to Jennifer.'

Dad said gently, 'I know, sweetheart, but you've

got to understand that, despite everything, Jennifer still has feelings of loyalty towards her mum.'

'Even though her mum *abandoned* her?'

Dad nodded. 'That's right.'

I thought about *my* mother then, and how I still had feelings of loyalty towards her, even though she'd gone and left me too – though in a different way. 'I suppose it's a bit like how I feel about *my* mum,' I said. Dad looked like he wasn't too sure what I meant so I added, 'I mean, I still feel like I should be loyal to her even though she isn't here and . . . and I do worry whether Lizzie minds that . . .' I trailed off.

After a few seconds, Lizzie asked quietly, 'Why do you think *I* would mind that, Esmie?'

'*If* you got married to Dad, I mean,' I added, flushing slightly. 'Because then you'd be . . . you know . . .'

The room was silent for several moments and I started to think I should learn to keep my feelings to myself in future. Lizzie was looking like she didn't know what to say.

Then Dad started talking slowly. 'Esmie, listen to me . . . Your mother was very special. She *can't* be replaced by anybody else. And neither can Lizzie. And it's the same for your feelings. The feelings you have for your mother won't be *replaced* by the ones you have for Lizzie. You're going to have feelings for Lizzie *and* feelings for your mum, and Lizzie knows that.'

I stared at Dad. I'd hardly heard him say anything about feelings before – Juliette always said that was partly because he was a man and partly because he was English – and here he was practically delivering a whole speech on the subject.

Lizzie was looking surprised too and her expression quickly changed to one of such warmth and . . . I don't know . . . *admiration* . . . that I suddenly felt like everything might be OK after all. And that even though Lizzie wanted a baby and Dad didn't, they *both* still wanted each other. And that maybe – just maybe – they could work things out without my help.

A few weeks later Dad asked me and Matthew how we'd feel about Lizzie moving in with us.

'Are you going to get married?' I asked him, thinking about how much I wanted to be a bridesmaid.

'We're going to try living together first,' Dad said. 'Then we'll see.'

'But does Lizzie still want a baby?' I asked him.

Dad looked at me sternly. 'Lizzie and I have been talking, Esmie, and we both agree that we'd like it if you didn't feel the need to have quite so much . . . information . . . about our relationship in future. And that includes issues about babies, OK?'

Matthew sniggered.

I scowled at my brother. 'I was only trying to help. Which is more than *you've* been doing!'

'Yeah, well, I've got my own girlfriend to think about, without worrying about Dad's,' he replied. Jennifer and Matthew were still seeing each other, but Jennifer was clearly much more interested in finding her mum than in anything else at the moment. And although Matthew was supporting her in that, I was pretty certain that he'd prefer to be at the top of Jennifer's list of priorities himself. (Holly had been horrified that Jennifer hadn't even gone with him to the hospital when he'd had his plaster cast removed, which she said just proved he needed a girlfriend who was more caring – like her.)

Jennifer and her aunt were currently waiting to hear back from some of her mother's old friends, who they had written to together and who they hoped might know where she was. But Jennifer had told me that even if she never found her mum, at least she was getting to know her Aunt Helen, thanks to me.

'So is Lizzie still going to see her therapist?' Juliette asked me when I phoned her to tell her about Lizzie moving in with us.

'Yes. She says she still finds it helpful, so she's going to keep going for a bit, despite what Dad thinks.'

'And what *does* your father think?'

'I don't know. When I asked him he said it was none of my business. But he *is* doing this one thing Lizzie asked him to do after her last session with Andrew. He's sorting out all the stuff in our loft.'

'Huh?'

'You know . . . all that stuff of my mum's that we've still got up there.'

'Ah . . . I see . . .'

'Oh and, Juliette, we're getting a kitten after all! Lizzie's getting one from someone at work and she's bringing it home with her this afternoon.'

'Wonderful!'

'It's a boy kitten so I want to call it Sherlock after Sherlock Holmes, or Hercule after Hercule Poirot, because they're my two favourite detectives.'

Juliette laughed. 'Are you still practising to be a detective yourself?'

'Yes, but I haven't got a case at the moment.'

'Well, if you are not busy, I was wondering, would you like to come and visit me in Paris for a weekend soon?'

'Oh, YES!' I yelled.

'But I do not want you looking for skeletons on the Champs-Élysées! Or chasing murderers up the *Tour Eiffel*! I just want us to go shopping, you understand. Nothing else.'

'Don't worry, Juliette. I promise I won't even bring my detective book with me,' I reassured her.

I heard the front door opening and Lizzie shouting, 'Come and see what I've got!'

'That's Lizzie with our kitten!' I told Juliette. 'I'll call you back later.'

I raced downstairs and got there just as Matthew was undoing the latches on the cat carrier that Lizzie had put down in the middle of the hallway.

'Careful, Matty. We don't want to scare it,' Dad said, standing just behind him. 'Just lift up the lid and let it stay in its box for now.'

I stepped closer to look inside the box. Huddled in the corner was this really small, cute black kitten with white paws – and when it looked up I saw that it had a white moustache.

'Hercule Poirot!' I announced immediately.

'Don't be daft, Esmie,' Matty snapped. 'You can't call him that!'

The kitten gave a little mew as I knelt down and gently put my hand out to stroke him. 'See,' I said, 'he likes his name. We can call him Hercule for short.'

Hercule let out an even louder miaow and got up on his hind legs to peer out over the side at us.

'He's certainly got a moustache like Hercule Poirot's,' Lizzie pointed out.

'Except it's white instead of black,' Matty said. 'And anyway, it isn't really a moustache.'

'Well, what do *you* want to call him then?' I snapped at my brother.

Matty just shrugged like he was far too cool to waste his time thinking up names for kittens. '*I* don't care.'

'In that case,' Dad said firmly, 'Hercule it is!'

I giggled. 'Now we've got *three* detectives in the family!'

Matthew let out a loud groan like he thought I was the most uncool sister anyone ever had, but I decided to let it pass. After all, when I grow up I'm going to be a *real* detective – and I'd like to see Matthew accuse me of not being cool *then*.